TINA ETHAIY

Torn

Contents

Prologue

Jess

Hiding in plain sight, I had been doing this for as long as I could remember, I was not on the run, I had done nothing illegal. No, my only crime was making the choice too… well that was the thing about it really, I hadn't made a choice. He had set me up, with something so innocent, I would never have dreamed, heck you would never have suspected either if you had been in my situation, such a simple question "Do you want to play hide and seek?"

Yup! A children's game played every day with so many of my peers of the time, I, myself just a child of five tender years then. How easy it was for him to ensnare me into his devilish world, a world that I remain attached too even today, all these years on. I should have stuck to my original answer of "No", definitely!

In hindsight, it was so out of his natural character at the time, his best mate and right hand as well. Together they strong armed me with such tenderness, gently pushing and persuading with their words for me to join in their innocent game.

How much I hated my younger self for changing her damn mind that day. Looking back at my younger self, in that checkered school uniform dress, and lime green hair band. Sitting on the steps outside the lunchroom, my lunch sitting heavy in my stomach, an open book in my lap, such pure innocence. Foolish girl, why did you allow his silver tongue to change your bloody mind? Close your book, refuse again, and walk away. That is how easy it could have been, but no, silly, foolish idiot I was, I agreed to play, and now I have no choice but to continue to play his game.

So, I hide in plain sight, always with the wall at my back, people think they know me, but in truth the people in my life today, have no idea of my past. My body is long broken, screams at me endlessly, doctors try pill after pill, perform test after test, trying to give my illness a name, but I already know the cause, it's him!

My body long ago tired of the games he plays, having lived on tender hooks for a lifetime, my body has given out, following my mind that he… correction they broke decades ago. I am sane, I promise you reader, I am the result of a lifetime of secrets, torture, and ownership. I live in a false freedom, that at any moment can be taken from me. I live by his rules and desires even today, he has proven that repeatedly over the years. The truth is, I am owned, and he has me addicted to his game!

Ron

"You're sure this time?" I questioned Stan, the club's investigator. 'Stan-the-Man' was very good at his job, I knew that. But I'd been given false leads before. She's gotten very good at disappearing over the last couple of decades. With the advancements in technology, she shouldn't be able to hide like she has, leaving no trace of herself, on the big world wide web and with only the barest of glimpses over the years on the dark net, she is extremely good at hiding her details from the world.

First, she'd turned my attention to the wrong continent, I'd spent more than I'd wanted trying to find her in mainland Japan and its tiny islands. Following ghostly leads, leaving behind paths paved with my money and powder.

Confirmations coming thick and fast in the beginning, loyalties and promises of friendship laced with her poison. Powerful combatants, aiding her and covering her tracks with lies. How she had bought their conviction to hide her, I still don't understand!

Then a glimpse of her confirmed in concrete, just as she left mainland Europe for the United States of America. But the destination eluded me. Fifty tiny and some not tiny at all, States, all wrapped up in that federally bound land. Following her trail like a game of peek-a-boo, my brothers in arms, have traveled the country from coast to coast, crisscrossing it like her personal puppets.

Stan hands me his photographic proof, with hands quaking with anger and desire, I study the face before me. She looks like her mother, her slender form transfigured in that chubby but not ugly shape of her mother. But it's her nose that tells me it's her alright, it's not long or bent like her mother's, no this is her father's nose, and it is her for sure.

My heart skipping, I switch to the second photo I held, pictured here, her grandchildren, and my weapon of choice for obedience. "Found you!" I whispered to myself. "She's been good at this for far too long, you're sure she's no idea you've tracked her?"

"Our brothers in South Carolina, assure me she has no idea these were taken. And thanks to the in-law connection we have everything you need."

Flipping back to the first photo, I stare into her face, memorizing the new details of that witch's face. "Leave the contact number on the desk." I was all too aware of the break in my voice, the emotions coursing through my veins, a power filled roller coaster of desire, pain and devilish joy at the conversation to follow.

Inhaling nicotine from the electric vape, I'd exchanged traditional cigarettes for; I shift my mindset to my last words to her. A deal had been made and she'd ultimately broken the deal with her disappearance. Surely, she'd understood the gift I'd given her, it was not license for her to run and hide like she has. She knew things were in place to keep her safe, she had agreed to be compliant, and then she'd taken off, become a bloody ghost!

Keeping that level of disgust forefront in my heart, I dialed the number before me. It rang and rang; I knew the number would not register on caller's details. Voice mail took over, pressing end, I dialed a second, third, fourth, fifth and sixth time, with no connection made.

Checking my watch, I did some basic mathematics. Time here minus time difference for there. Early evening her time, she's home alone per the schedule of her movements, Stan has included in his documentation.

"Pickup!" I spit to the empty room. Thumbing through my email, I found Stan's latest, he'd sent it after our meeting as instructed. At the bottom, three photos are attached.

The first; a copy of the closeup I have of her face in front of me, the other two of the grandchildren and her daughter's family. Downloading the family pictures to the phone, I make light work of attaching them to a clipped text message to her mobile phone, "Answer your phone. RB" I allow time for the message to arrive and then check the info of my sent message, it's been delivered.

I give the unstated acknowledgment that I can reach the people she loves a little more time, pouring myself a brandy, I allow my palm to heat the liquid trapped in my glass. Soon I'd warm something else I promised myself, she'll reap the rewards of the seeds she's sown and pay the toll, of her travels. I'd long stopped counting the pain I'd deal, but now with her within my reach again, I started to mentally tally up the cost of her deceit.

Taking the final drop of the smooth brandy from the glass, I temper my feelings as I once again hit redial on the burner. I count the rings as I envision her weighing her decision to answer the unknown caller.

"Really?" her voice holds contempt for the way I was demand her compliance. I allow her energy to fill me, even with the distance and the technology between us, I felt the faint singe of her power. Seconds tick one by one slowing the beat of my own heart. "You went to great lengths to waste it on silence."

Her statement breaking her spell, I take a deep inhale of nicotine once more. "If I didn't..." I trail away from words like love "would you have answered?" Now it's her turn to remain silent, and I allow her to simmer in it. We are both no doubt in that place once again, where hate is no stranger.

We'd been so young, and so unprepared for the things in our near future. I'd been instructed to make her mine, I didn't understand what was necessary, she was just a girl, and I? Just a boy. Both of us children, both of us uneducated in the things that would be expected of us. I would call her my girl and she'd call me boyfriend. Neither of us understand the labels further than the facts of our individual, sexual identifiers, of girl and boy.

"Look, let's start over..." I suggest with cold hearted, kindness lacing my "Hello Babe!"

"Hi" her response "Fine! You win! Now what? I trust there is some purpose to this call, what is it you want?" the emotion in voice, building like a storm crashing inland as she punctuates the final question.

"I've missed you" I begin, ignoring her rage, knowing that I'm just stoking her flames. "What!?"

"Sorry, is the connection not good?" I provoke "I miss you" I repeat softly.

"I answered, I'm not playing your stupid game?"

She wants information, details for the call, not reminiscence of our past moments, but I want her, the real her, my girl, not this version of the club witch, bitter with time and memories that just maybe betray her.

"It's called a conversation; you remember how that works right? I say something, you respond in kind. Let's try this again, I say Hello, I miss you, and you something nice, you remember right? You remember, us?"

"You threatened what's mine! For conversation? Seems like a high price, you lonely big man?"

I chuckled at her words, allowing her to hear the rumble in response to her words, before inhaling unnecessarily loudly for the effect "Like I said I've missed you."

A board smile stretching over my heavily stumbled face. Another intake of nicotine. "I'm too old for your games! Ronald Baker!"

"I'll never be too old to miss you, Princess." I changed the word love to miss just as the words left my lips "Is it too much to ask for a little memory lane and gentle conversation, must our first words after all this time be laced with threats and pain? Don't answer that, I can already feel the charge you're sending."

"The fact is, I do in fact miss your companionship, we both have families and lives we've lived without the other, I was hoping for some civility and a moment of past reflection. Before we talk of obligation."

Jess

L istening to the calmness in his voice is infuriating, he holds all the cards once again, I'm on his time, at his mercy once more, before he does more than take pictures. How'd he'd find me? I'm unsure, I'd been so careful, hiding in plain sight, different names for social profiles, acting like an ordinary person.

I'd not pulled on my power in years, I knew the Watchers could find me quickly if I pulled on the energy around me. And now I'm stuck listening to him, telling me how he's missed my company, oh I have no doubt he's missed me, but it isn't my company he's missed! It's the power I allow him to present by having me at his side.

"Memories you say. The memories I have aren't sweet and cuddly, so excuse me if I'd rather leave them where they belong, like you, in my past! Long forgotten and never given a moment's thought." I take pause enough to sense his anger "You want to reflect? Be civil? and yet you start this whole thing with the implied endangerment of those that I do love! And care about. We had an agreement, you do remember, right…"

"Do you!?" he demands; Now the truth, in his words exploding from under the thin veil of pleasant reunification "You ran! You went into hiding, our agreements words still drying in the sand!"

"Dust to dust!"

"Death will not come by my hand for you, Witch! You are mine! You will always be mine! Time hasn't changed that!"

No, I hadn't forgotten those words, I'd begged for my freedom, but he'd never give me that, I'd always be his, he'd made that clear repeatedly, even the agreement had made that clear.

"Naturally!" I state, both as an acknowledgment of his ownership and the only way this would end for me. Mother nature would be my only way out. He'd do everything he could to make sure that my life was a very long one. It's at that thought that I wonder if he knows just how sick I am, is that why he has made the reconnection? After all, he would lose a unique tool when I die.

"Look, I never wanted a fight, that's why I thought this would be the least threatening way for us to reconnect. I've been looking for you a long time, I never meant for us to fight, I do miss you, all of you not just your gifts, I miss your smile, your wit, I miss you being by my side during hard times. It's hard times right now, and your return to me feels fated. I'm asking you for a new beginning."

I didn't have to hide my location anymore, so I pull from the universe and there I found him. Christopher Baker, the creator of my tormentor. Ron's much older brother. He's a faint image, so newly crossed into the ether.

"If it's my sorrow you expect for your loss, you've knocked on the wrong door." I allow my words to sting, his temper and soul be damned. I won't mourn the loss of his brother.

"Of course not, but it does seem the timing Is fated, he's barely cold and your details come in the same week."

The powers that be, always using me for death, it is however surprising that I've had no warning about Christopher's departure from the living. I could only assume that the shields I've placed around the important people in my life has also separated me from those that claim ownership.

"Look, I'm sorry, okay? Maybe we can come to a new agreement, one that allows us our own space, solidifies things between us for the future?" His words come slowly; it's obvious he's choosing them carefully.

"You want to negotiate?" I respond. All my inner

alerts exploding with this change in conversational direction.

"I'll let you keep what you consider to be yours, and you in return will answer my calls and help the family as needed?" His proposal has so many loopholes, all in his favor it seems.

"Keep what's mine? You'll not touch or hurt them in any way, let me correct that. You and yours or anyone employed by you or yours will not touch or hurt those I claim as my own?" I'd long ago learned that when making deals with the Devil you needed to be very precise with your wording.

"You'll need to send me a list of names, I'll not agree to that open statement, as well you know." He retorts. Still, he hasn't given any restrictions on the number of people listed. "And in return you'll answer my calls, be polite and assist as needed." He changed the terms in his repetition of his side to the deal. "Furthermore, should it be necessary, you will adjust your life for our safety."

"I'll agree to answer your phone calls in return for what's mine, but you'll need to be specific with that 'Adjust my life part'? To be clear I'm not agreeing to that until you put parameters around just what the adjustment would look like."

I hear him chuckle yet again, fucking wanker! He's having fun toying with my future with his words. Maybe I'd been better off with Christopher as the head of the family, Ron is far too clever with his words. Don't get me wrong, Chris was one twisted son of a bitch, but his words never held secrets or lies, what he said, he did, plain and simple. Ron on the other hand, loves deals made with empty statements and open-ended conclusions. My clarifications of my own words, seemingly redundant to this conversation are necessary to stop the unintended acceptance without rebuttal to statements clear. "Well, that would be situational, hard to put parameters around an unknown quantity, Princess."

Fucker! "Then we are at an impasse, unless you want to say you agree to what's mine is mine and I'll answer your phone calls when necessary?"

"Or we scrap this conversation and I'll be seeing you soon?"

Could I take off again, leave my ever-growing family behind me, destroy those who love me. I didn't have any funds to run with, I'd cut all my past connections and spent any favors long ago. Then where would I go? With Chris dead, Ron would have nothing stopping him from tearing this planet apart to get to me, then everyone would pay for my disappearance.

"Princess?"

"If adjustments need to be made, what's mine will never know and any minders will not be welcome as house guests?" It is a hail-Mary; made with regret the moment the words are given voice. But he has me trapped and we both knew it.

"Deal! The list is due at once, you have today's phone number. Sweet Dreams Princess."

He didn't wait for my reply, just ended the call with his words still processing in my head. What had I just done? You stupid little girl! I stew in self-hatred, until I'm interrupted by a single worded text message. "List".

I start listing everyone by first and last name, which are currently or have been in my life at some point since I've left home and the them. If I don't remember their full name, I add a location or other identifier. Then I list places, every place I can remember ever being, during the years I've run free and anyone to do with those places.

The list is several text messages long, he wanted a list, I'd give him one that includes every living soul that's ever looked or even thought to look in my direction, no physical weapons with a breath will be available to him.

I list people in places, he thought loyal, knowing that the betrayal will hit him personally. He who lied so well and so often didn't care for the same in return. Finally, I sent "End of List" as a confirmation of the task completed. I receive no reply. Sleep does not come easy or sweetly to me either.

Jess

Putting Ron and his world back into my memory box, of things and people I don't need in my everyday life, is difficult over the next few weeks. Sleep only comes when I was completely exhausted, flashes of the past creep into my dreams, memories long sealed away, speckled nightmares of things that never happened. Waking hours aren't any better, my eyes and mind playing evil tricks on me, catching glimpses of non-existent people, jumping at the all too familiar sounds of motorbikes going by.

The first time I venture over to visit with my grandchildren, I scan the area, trying to figure out where the photographer had been that took the photos he'd sent to me. How close had they been to get the pictures? Were they safe now? So many places would allow them to watch my loved one's coming and going, without anyone realizing anything was amiss.

Would Ron keep to the guidelines we'd agreed

on? I certainly didn't last time we came to an arrangement; I'd not even waited twenty-four hours before setting up a false trail for him to follow. Would he be vengeful and do more than watch them? My youngest is so damn beautiful, would he take her? Would he discover she's a witch as well? I send a silent prayer into the ether for her protection.

Walking into my daughter's home, both grandchildren tackled me on at the open door, I push them gently inside, relieved to see her husband home. As a self-proclaimed Redneck, Jace knows how to handle himself well. Being with them brings me comfort and peace of mind. The kids involve me in their game of monopoly, which I lose. And I get to put them to bed, with kisses. Naturally having Nana visiting means that we have to repeat the 'go to bed' ritual several times. Hanging out with them until darkness of night starts to fall, helps to reset my brain.

I'd been fixated on the phone call, the past and Ron for far too long. It is time to really get back to being Nana a fifty-one-year-old, with too many dogs, a loving husband and an ever-growing family. Driving the few miles home that night, I finally allow the tension I've carried with me, since the phone call to dissipate. Christopher is dead, and I'd bury him, Ron and the past in my memories of things not to think about.

Getting home in time to greet my husband, we fall into bed together, wrapped in his loving arms, I kiss him goodnight, close my eyes and allow peaceful sleep to finally overtake me.

Waking up to the alarm, I thank Goddess, for a restful night's sleep, today is a workday, so I turn the shower on, giving it a few minutes to warm up, and get in. The water is steaming and beats down with just the right amount of pressure, to massage my neck muscles. I tilt my back into the water, staying there just long enough to shampoo and condition my head after getting dressed I head for the kitchen.

The Keurig is a wonderful invention. Coffee in minutes that doesn't suck like instant coffee, a quick scramble egg and muffin complete today's breakfast.

Arriving at the office, I park to the side of the building in my regular spot. Double checking, as is standard for me, that the doors are locked, I join a few other employees making their way into the building. Cindy is kind enough to punch in her door code, and hold the door open for everyone, we all line up to punch in on the time card machine outside the break room. While they go into the break room, I head for my office, which I share with two other ladies, Mickey and Rachel, together we make up the checkout team.

Dumping my bag under the desk, I start where I'd left of on Friday. Working nine to five, no weekends is close to my dream job as I could get. It's easy work, making referrals and scheduling appointments. In the afternoon, the doctors will start to see patients and we'll switch gears to checking out today's appointments. I always try to make patients giggle while spending their money and try to get follow ups and outpatient appointments set up before they left the building.

Soon enough, my life had returned to normal, the phone conversation a dusty memory, locked away tightly in a memory box, marked never open. The everyday routine of work and home interrupted occasionally by doctors' visits or fun times hanging out with family.

That is until the middle of May, I'm heading to my car with Mickey when she comments "I wouldn't mind that!" She's pointing towards a guy leaning against a motorcycle, parked next to my car. His long, jet black hair falling below his Polo shirt collar, black jeans and Doc Martins completing his outfit.

"Jess?" his deep voice calls out as we get closer.

"Yum!" exclaims Mickey "You gonna introduce me?" She is giddy for the handsome image before us. "Trust me, you don't want any of that. See you later girl." I tried to dismiss her, but she runs on up to tall dark and handsome. As I drag my own feet, knowing I don't want to make contact any quicker.

Terry doesn't miss a trick, straightening his stance, he folds his arms, in a non-verbal no nonsense gesture. "Not tonight sweetheart." He notes to Mickey as she reaches him a full length ahead of me.

"See you tomorrow, Mickey" I tell her as I walk up to her shoulder "trust me, he's not for you!"

Turning Mickey mouths "Call me!" before calling out "Goodnight hansom" to Terry and walking away towards her car.

"Spoil sport" he goads me, once Mickey's out of earshot.

I pull my mobile phone from my back pocket and make a big deal of checking that it is in fact turned on and in working order "Appears to be in working order, so?" I leave the implied question hanging, he's a smart man, he knows why.

Ron's agreement has lasted a little over six months, he'd agreed he'd call, but here I stand with my minder standing less than an arm's length in front of me.

Terry really is a nice guy at heart, he's walked the grey line for me more than once in the past, but then that was when we'd been much younger, and he'd the 'hots' for me. He'd also been a great nursemaid after I'd taken a beating at Ron's hands. To me he has always been like that annoying little brother, no one wanted hanging around.

"Do I get a hug?" he asks, opening his arms wide to me while reaching forward to snag me into his embrace. He knows I hate physical contact when I don't initiate it, but I don't fight it. It's been years after all, since we'd shared the same air. Breathing in the familiar scent of his cologne, I have to admit to myself I've missed him. He is warm, and safe.

We both lingered in the embrace longer than a friendly hello. "So, you gonna follow me or is my bike safe here?"

"How long is this going to take, I'm expected at home?"

With disappointment in his tone "Really! You going to lie to me?"

I shrug my shoulders "Worth a try, okay I'll follow you, but my husband gets off at nine tonight, so…" "Guess I'm leaving my bike here, then! Keys!"

I drop the keys from my hand into his waiting palm "I said I'd follow you." I complain like a petulant child. "Yeah! And you've lied to me twice now." He nods for me to walk to the passenger side of my car.

"Fine!" giving in as I stroll around the front of my car to the other side. Getting in, I tug at the seat belt, fixing it into place. My work bag thrown into the back seat, Terry adjusts the driver's seat and mirrors. Annoying me further, at least my husband

and I don't have to make adjustment's when we drive each other's cars. It will take ages to get the settings back the way I like them.

"I would have followed you."

"Sure, you would." his tone reaps of disbelief and sarcasm, not that I really blamed him. I hook up my phone to the car stereo system, and Whitesnake's "Here we go again" comes on.

Terry reaches over and turns the volume up. "Very appropriate" he chuckles. Then he reverses out of the parking spot and heads towards the interstate.

We are at least headed in the direction of home, driving in silence, the music shifts from soft metal to country, "God's country" by Blake Shelton is playing as we enter the not so safe, local neighborhood. I have cop friends that have told me they wouldn't enter this area without backup. Given the company the I'm currently keeping, I'm surprised as we head into this area.

Several turns later we're pulling into the front yard of an average single-story home. Several motorbikes are parked on the lawn area, and I spot a 1970's Chevelle SS parked in the car port. Cars are a hobby of mine, from the front this one looks to be well cared for, if it has been kept in its original state it is worth well over hundred-twenty thousand, but then I notice some idiot has lifted it and stuck it on outrageous tires. Such a shame. "Damn!" I exclaimed as we passed.

"Huh?" Terry questions, and then "Oh! Yes Americans!" shaking his head in disapproval at the tires with me.

From this moment on he's the enemy I remind myself, taking a quick tally of the bikes outside, this little house is going to be brimming with monsters. I gather in the ether's energy around me, with every step closer to the entrance. I need to shield myself from their stupidity.

Walking through the doorway, I feel my shields form, taking shape around me. I spot a familiar young face in the crowded hallway, it's obvious to me that no one had instructed these fools to give me space as I enter. Static electricity sparks between me and several of them as we pass.

We hear "What the fuck!" as the third guy gets a particularly high voltage shock.

"Make way" Terry orders from behind me.

"Jess! Play nice." Comes a second louder voice from within the first room to my right.

Several responses flip through my mind, but I hold my tongue; now is the time for silence as silence holds so much more power. No matter how much I want to chide him and the situation he is putting me in. Here I need to keep control of my words and protect my secrets. Now is not the time for Ron or anyone else to discover that my magick is so much more than it has ever been in the past. Now it is game on, and I have to stay calm, this is his world I remind myself as I enter the room Ronald waits in.

"Gonna need to collect my ride, Guv!" Terry announced without further explanation before heading back out.

"Seriously?" The smirk on Ron's face gives him away, he hadn't expected me to come without complaint. Ignoring him, I assess the room from just inside the doorway, the wall to my right is lined with what could only be described as cheap plastic lawn chairs. Ron and three other men sit opposite where I stand on the other side of the room, on bar stools. A battered sofa under the double windows, looks out towards the road, several men gathered in tiny huddles throughout the room.

The wall to my left is basically void of anything or anyone, so I take a step in that direction, uncomfortable with the open doorway behind me. I am midway into my next step when Ron clears his throat, obviously gesturing for my attention.

Game on! Did I play 'Simon Says' or say, 'fuck it'? and see what happens.

Yes, everything is a game here in his world, sometimes the rules are clear and other times, like now the rules are not well defined but the power exchange between us, always dancing a fine line, of me keeping him happy or paying the price for pushing him too far.

I stare at him, and weigh my options, staying as I am, the open door remains behind me, not knowing who or what might creep up behind me makes me uncomfortable so should I continue to the wall area in front of me? The briefest of moments have me deciding to surprise him, I walk directly over to him, drop to my knees in front of him, placed my hands in my lap and bow my head.

This position is one of total submission, and I can feel his surprise. Waiting for his next move, I note the change in the atmosphere around me, all conversation has stopped, the weight of eyes on me growing heavy. I remain motionless, taking calm breaths as slow movement begins again, some leave the room entirely, others assume residence on a chair or the couch. A handful up against the wall, I would have preferred over my current position.

Ron and I both know that I've taken his power by deciding to take control over my submission. Saving us both the struggle in front of an audience. Even in this position, I am winning. Kneeling in the silence, I relax, my shield is wrapped around me like a soft blanket. The only emotional vibes I allow to pass my shield are his. I need to keep those so I can be ready for his attack, should that be his decision.

Ron

Seeing Jess kneeling in front of me, like she'd done a thousand times before, surprises me. It did make my position a little stronger in appearance to have her give her submission without command or fighting, I know better than to think I've won.

I know she's watching the movement in the room; she's calculating everyone's position in the pack. The locals in the room standing against the wall, already discounted as possible threats. Judging by the noise of those in the hallway, I also know she's holding a vast amount of ether power in her body. I'm unsure if she's aware of the company I'm keeping, it's their meeting.

The Kings, their official title, are the top dogs in the room. They control all the business, of the all the clubs across three continents. It's their party now, I let her sit in silence.

Jess

Shiny shoes enter my field of vision, the crisp pleat on his trousers hover above the shoe purposely. From the length of the shoe, I guesstimate the owner of the shoes to be the slightly slender man, I spotted standing next to Ron as I approached them before kneeling. "You don't fool me Witch" he proclaims, "Look at me when I speak to you."

I ignore his command as Ron and I are still playing.

A second individual steps next to the first, this one's wearing black trainers and matching jeans. "Chris told me; Ron would not be a good choice as guardian for you, and it would appear he is right, kneeling there as you are, you do not fool me!"

This second man isn't wasting time waiting for a response, as he prowls around my position and steps outside of my line of sight.

"Prove us wrong, young Ron, take the chains." A third, older voice with an accent I can't place speaks the words I fear the most.

I know a dead man, can't hold the chains, but I foolishly thought that since Ronald has been my guardian all these years, he'd not have to go through the ritual of taking them from his brother. I'd only been five when Chris had forced my true form into the realm of the living; in truth I don't remember much about that day.

"Francis, Jess and I have been a bonded pair fair too long for the theatrics of the past, I understand Chris had opinions he shared with you, he shared the same with me. He is wrong!"

Listening to Ron's words, flat and void of emotion. His words for the room, not just this older stranger.

"Then why do you not hold the chains already? Chris could have given them to you anytime, and yet he saw fit to take them with him into death?"

"My brother never shared his toys even when we were kids, why would you think he'd give them away?" Ron's retort is coated in truth and exasperation.

Chris was addicted to the power of my energy, when we were close enough for him to steal it. That's one reasons I've put so many miles between us and wrapped myself in a permanent shield of protection from him. I'd had that shield in place so long, it as much a part of me as breathing.

The conversation is getting repetitive, and is going downhill, Ron's looking weaker by the second.

During all of this, I remain silent, motionless as if I'd become a statue. Pins and needles creeping along my lower limbs, stiffness forming in my bowed neck. I listen without fidgeting. Soon enough words would be replaced with commands, I'd give them no reason to speed things along.

"Fine! Let's ask him!"

"Jess?" How many times Ron had called my name, I did not know, but I felt his anger vibrate through his hand as he taps me on the back of the head. "Jess? Are you sleeping?"

"No, just giving you privacy." I respond truthfully, without looking up at him.

"They want to speak to Chris."

Summoning the newly deceased is more complicated since the newly departed don't know how to hold their own form. It's common for the ghost to appear translucent and show gruesome details of how they were as the life drained from them. Even though it has been several months, I doubt Chris has spent much time trying to become seen.

I know he's still tied to this world, he holds my chains, I doubt even now he'd give those up easily. I'd figured their conversation was going to lead to this request, last time I peeked into the ether for him, he'd not registered the contact, still new to his new circumstance and death. Contrary to the common belief that the dead hang around the living all day, I knew he could be unwilling to join us.

Lifting my head, I offer Ron my hand, in a silent request to aid me in standing. I'd not face Chris on my knees. Mr. Trainers reaches forward to help me. Looking at Ron, I wait for permission. With a casual nod of his head, I take Mr. Trainer's hand, the spark that jumped from my palm to his fingers illuminate the immediate area, as a light bulb does just as it bursts. "Tut, tut!" he expresses it without pause to the pain, I knew I'd just sent him. Tightening his grip around my hand, he raises me to my feet.

Demon eyes reflect my image as I take in his elderly features. Seeing past the glamour of his human features, rough, blackened scales replace wrinkles of the old man before me. Ivory tucks protrude from his lower lip and horns poke out above his eyebrows. I pull my hand free the moment I stand straight.

This King is a Demon, I wonder what the others are. Ignoring Ron, I reached out into the ether and check the energy pouring from the other two Kings in the room, a bear growls at me, from within the smartly suited gentleman and the stink of death pours out of the third. Surprise must have shone across my face, as I take in this information, turning to Ron I couldn't help my words.

"Demon, Bear-Shifter and Vampire, you really are

fucked!"

"And Witch, Princess" he clarified with pride "Don't forget the Witch, after all you are the main prize!" "You want Christopher!" Anger at his words exploding from me, I pulled Chris into being, Chris shimmers into view, then whirls on me. His mouth is moving, but no sound comes. I laugh out loud.

"You're in my world now!" I reply to his cursing form.

In reply, he pulls on my energy, I'm not ready to give it to him, a gasp escapes my lips, as Chris takes solid form unexpectedly, I feel an unfamiliar burn around my left wrist, looking down, I see flames licking around a manacle I don't remember seeing before.

"How dare you!" he bellows, my energy fueling his corporal form.

I grab at my burning wrist, only to discover my right is also manacled, rage burning between both of us, my struggle only giving weight to the chains that are now visible between us, for the second time in my life. My mind closes around the pain, looking down in panic.

"Settle down Witch!" a voice in the distance calls out.

The flames lick at my arms and torso now, I'm being consumed by Christopher's rage, I must let him go, but how? I can't think as the pain consumes me. Crashing to the floor; stop, drop and roll comes to mind.

"Shield your fucking self!" The command cuts into my pain, it's Ron.

The flames burn blue, as Christopher seems to take in his own surroundings, I must get a handle on the situation, but the flames are just intensifying.

"Shields!" comes Ron's command again "Damn it! I knew she wasn't ready…" his voice trails off into the distance.

Shield, I tried to focus on my shield, its crystal edging encircles both of us. It wavers in the distance, as the flames turn orange once again. A scream fills my lungs, as Christopher's image gets close and personal in my space.

"You will always be mine." he proclaims, "you're still that weak little girl?"

My breathing ragged, I feel myself shrink, as my younger self emerges from within.

"Stop!" I cry inwardly, I can hear screaming in the distance, as he displays the familiar face of sick enjoyment.

"Princess, look at me" comes the gentle whisper of Ron's voice "I need you to shield." Ronald comes into focus for the barest flicker of time. "Daddy?" I reply as his image evaporates. "Yes, Princess, Shields up!"

Christopher, laughs into my face "Mine!"

I take the anger that word produces and just like that, my shields snap into place and Christopher finds himself contained in his own private bubble of hell. Taking from the ether wildly, I pour all the pain he's given back into him, becoming aware that the chains that bind me, also bind him to me. Revenge is mine, still reeling in his punishment I return everything he's given me over a lifetime into those chains, his evil flames now traveling in his direction, I stoke the fire with the hatred I have for him.

"Stop!" Ron Commands.

"My turn" I proclaim, my throat roaring with pain.

"No!" Ron takes hold of my chin, raising my face to force me to focus on him "Jessica, I command you to Stop." His grip firm, he holds my attention.

Seconds tick on a nonexistent clock as my heartbeat slows "Vengeance is mine, not yours!" his eyes hold my attention, I swear he can see inside my soul.

"I will talk to my brother now." My eyes lock on his, his hand still firm on my chin.

I make the slightest of nodding gestures to signal my agreement. "Give me your hand" raising my right hand slowly, he takes it with his free hand, if it is still charged, he gives no outward sign of pain.

"Good girl." Releasing my chin, helping me back into a standing position, his brother still encased in my bubble, I raise my left hand allowing it to break the surface of the bubble that contains Christopher.

Ron reaches out with his other hand now, in the same general direction as my left. I watch as Christopher takes his hand, with the connection made I remove my protective bubble completely. "Why, Brother?" Ron's first question.

"You'll need to more specific." Christopher replies, his volume a little too loud. He is still adjusting. "She is Mine!"

"And now she's going to be mine, release her!"

"You're weak, and she knows it! You're not worthy, you never were!"

"Worthy enough to protect and command her all these years?" Ron counters.

"Your love for her makes you weak, you can never control her."

I want to burn him, try to melt the chains from around my limbs, but I'd heard the story of another that had tried and failed. So, I do the only thing I can think of and start to pour my power into Ron. Giving him the strength of Hercules.

"They are little more than paper for you now Ron! Break the chains." I channel more energy into him with every word.

"They are mine to give, not his!"

"Take them!" Where that knowledge has come from, I don't know, but I know it to be true. They were mine to give and his to take. Christopher realizes the truth of my words, his form shivering with rage.

"He's no match for you, Witch!" Christopher spits.

Stepping closer, I feel my wings expand behind me, as I shed my corporal form, lifting off the ground a few inches, still holding the connection between the brothers and myself.

"Ronald Baker" I name my new guardian "Take your right hand and take the chains." I command.

Ron does as I instruct, throwing caution to the wind, his right hand takes ahold of the chain between Christopher and myself.

The chain changes shape as he does, a serpent bites into his wrist and then wraps itself around it. A second serpent bites his other wrist and does the same. The chains that had connected me to Christopher transform, I am finally free of Christopher, the moment I have dreamed of, has finally come true. I can no longer feel his hold over me. And now vengeance is mine.

"No!" comes the order "Princess you are better than that." Ron's eerily calm comment freezing thoughts of vengeance. "Let him go, Princess. It's time to just let him go."

Indecision tears through me, I want Chris to suffer, but the calmness Ron is pouring into me, has me wanting his warm embrace.

Floating back towards the ground, I note my slumped empty body lying on the floor below. I remembered being outside myself once before. This body is older, damaged with time and illness, I release my hold on Ron's remaining hand and swoop into my empty shell.

"You must me kinder to us both Guardian." I mutter as I enter.

"You are both beautiful, but I never expected wings, your true form is amazing." Ron replies in awe.

"Be kinder, new master, than the last and I will make things right" My inner self replies as we become one once more.

Jess

Waking in a bed that's not mine, in a room that smells of dirty laundry. I lay shaking uncontrollably, with distant voices coming from a direction I can't pinpoint.

"Don't try to move, take your time." A hand brushes my hair away from my face, it's smooth and soft. I try to open my eyes, but the light is too bright and stings them like a hot poker.

"Get her something to drink." comes another voice that is strangely familiar. A young man, I think.

Why can't I stop trembling? I muse and then it all comes crashing back. I'd separated from my body for a second time. I remember shaking non-stop after the first time, but I'd thought that was because of what they'd done to me, not because she had taken me to safety. Had my grandmother come again, had she protected me like last time, had she been here. My confused mind flitters from fact to fiction, from past to present, and back again.

"Take your time, just breathe" the first voice suggests, a cold damp softness wipes across my brow. "Here!" a third offered.

Goddess! I hope that's not a stupid glass of water! I exclaimed internally. I remembered sitting there, propped up against the refrigerator, in that tiny kitchen, legs swinging to my left. Water splashing from the glass I couldn't hold steady in my hands.

My mind whirling, but I'm in bed, not sitting with my bottom on cold flooring. What is that foul smell? Dirty laundry? I crack my eyes, just a little, that's not so painful now, opening them fully, a female unfamiliar to me, comes into view. It's her wiping my forehead with that cool towel. Her voice reminding me to breathe.

"Everyone out!" she instructs the room, feet shuffled from the room. "Give me that! " She barks at someone.

Then I see the mug, as she sets it down on the table beside my pillow. "Out!" comes her voice again. "You take your time dear; I've set Tylenol and drink for you here on the table. You don't need them or me fussing over you now."

I nod, but a sharp pain hits me between the eyes that has me closing them once more. "Remember deep breaths and take your time."

With that I'm left alone, in this room that smells of stale laundry.

Ron

Hold up in this neighborhood, a strange combination of a council estate that is privately owned, I tire of the Kings company. Francis continues to mutter that I'm not worthy and can't maintain the power she holds.

Baron has softened, he like Francis has seen the chains taken before but proclaims the serpents are a new one on him. He's taken to researching the phenomenon, searching for a reason for the unusual turn of events.

Hank has taken root next to Jessica, in the corner of the small bedroom down the hall.

It's been days, I've been texting her husband from her mobile, as far as he knows, she's been sent for software training in California. I've had a few random photos of the coast sprinkled over her Facebook timeline.

Her younger daughter keeps trying to video chat, it's getting increasingly difficult to fob her off. I studied their earlier conversations to do my best to mimic their daily text chats. Much longer, and I'd have to have her brought here. Jessica would be furious and the damage that might do to this very tentative situation would be unhealthy.

Relief rolls over me, when Tabitha announces to me that Jessica is finally awake. I'd worried the serpent thing had done permanent damage. Following Tabitha's instruction to keep my distance is infuriating, it's not like I'm ever going to do that to her again. I'm still adjusting to the connection between us, watching her nightmares and dreams while I'm sleeping is surreal.

I have my own memories from those early days. I know the pain I'd caused her but seeing it like a movie from her point of view shows me what a gruesome bastard I truly am! If I'd been her, I don't think I'd still be living. And then there are reels not familiar to me, pain caused by those that claimed to be family, that claimed to love her.

Outside of those clips, there are the clips of the dying, among those a clip I'd experienced yesterday, of a young soldier, kneeling in a building missing its roof, doors, with windows void of glass. The floor covered in debris, his friend kneeling in front of him. Three other guys in the room, one guarding the young soldier whose body I seemed to occupy, holds a gun on me. Another stands behind my friend and the third is obviously in charge of the threesome. A shot rings out and I watch my friend fold forward, lifeless. As I reach out a second shot rings out. I feel nothing at first, then I tumble uncontrollably forward myself, although I don't feel my landing, warm liquid spills out of the corner of my mouth, its metallic taste coating my tongue and then I am awake. Back in myself, checking my own bloody neck for the bullet wound, that isn't there.

I'm lying on the sofa in the front room, I remind myself it isn't real, my connection with Jessica is gone now I'm awake. I know she sees death coming, but to see it for myself the way she sees it is unbelievably disturbing.

I wonder if Christopher has seen the things I am seeing, pouring out of her while she sleeps. I recall the day he took her chains; she had passed out then as well, but only for a few minutes. Thomas had scooped her up and taken her into the kitchen. From the clips Jess had shown me, he'd placed his tee shirt on her, it's unclear to me how she ended up sitting on the floor, the kitchen table in front of her and the chair tucked under it within reach. The details are immaculate, the dullness of the metallic chair legs, the yellow checkered tablecloth of my childhood covering what I know to be a well-worn tabletop. Adrenaline coursing through her, she couldn't control her trembling.

"Hank's still keeping watch." Tabitha announces

"I'm going to take my leave now, nothing else I can do for her now. It might still be a few days before she's fully recovered, don't rush her. She'll come to you when she's ready." With a respectful curtsy to Francis, the vampire blinks out of the room.

"Tell me more about the connection?" Baron asks for the thousandth time as he reenters the front room "What does it feel like? Can you taste, smell? You said it's in full color, but I need more."

Shrugging, I run my hand through my hair, rerunning the clip of the young soldier "It's a movie… no it's more…Didn't Chris ever explain it? It's as real as it for us to be here in this room."

"Your connection with her is different, if Chris saw these things he never said."

I need to talk to Jess, I pace the room, impatience growing within me. "I'm going for a ride." I announce, not waiting for permission, exiting the house, I signaled for Terry to follow.

Mounting the borrowed Harley, I kick it into gear and head for the main road I'd come to know as Bluff. I head away from the city, I don't have a destination in mind, just needing to ride. Terry shadows me as we ride the road to its end, turning in a random direction, I follow the fields and trees that line the country road, at every intersection I take another random direction, forty or fifty minutes later we are following signs for a state park called

Santee.

Pulling up to the entrance hut, Terry pulls up beside me "Pay the man."

As money exchanged hands, I pull away, following the trail to lands' end. It opens on a large body of water, the area void of any two-legged forms, Terry hot on my heels.

"Hey that guy warned of gators! There's fucking dinosaur's here Guv!" he tells me as I dismount my ride. "What?"

"Alligator's! Hundreds of them!"

"Huh, interesting." I returned unfazed. As Tel hands me a map of the area. Scanning it, I don't see any alligator's pictured, like I expect an area marked on the tourist map. "Stay with the bikes, I need to clear my head, Mate!"

I wander down, through the fence and along a well-worn path. The water splashes along the edge where it meets land. I'd wander over towards the edge, it was a fair way down, the path winding around, I end in a clearing of mowed grass. The track seems to peak up, and goes over the edge, I change direction and take my time heading back towards the bikes.

What was I doing out here? I should have put Jess on a plane by now and been walking familiar streets back home, not wondering where the Alligators are. My life is so fucked up! Vampires, shifters, Demons and Witches!

Seeing Jessica, the day Chris had first pulled her true form forward, seeing her bright, golden angel-like form float above her young broken body, I'd been forced into a world of fantasy. Thomas, who as it turned out is a young vampire belonging to Francis's clan. I say young but he told me he was over one hundred human years on that day. How old Francis was then and is today even, I can only guess, he is certainly hundreds of years older than Thomas.

My Dad's small club became part of a much more powerful worldwide club that day. Apparently, Witches are a part of Jessica's family tree. The Watcher's, a group of different other worldly species keep track of these things, seeing the opportunity to enslave Jessica at a young age. A plan was devised, and my brother was named as Guardian, as he, unlike Dad was not addicted to any substance.

As for me, I was charged with controlling her, when we were at school, and then outside of school. If she wasn't with her family, she was with ours. I followed my dad's lead and treated her the same way, he and Chris treat the females in their lives. She'd do as I tell her or she'd feel my disapproval, it is only now, seeing it from her point of view, how crazy living like that had made our relationship. It's no wonder she and I had gotten to the point we had before our original agreement, and then she'd ran. Shit I would have gone further, I'd seen where she'd tried to take her own life a few times, each time coming up with reasons to remain living.

She loved and loved hard! Putting the pain of others in front of her own. Accepting the punishments, I doled out, expecting the unexpected aggression, I'd grown easy expressing towards her.

"Set the sat-nav back, I'll follow you" I tell Terry as I mount the bike once more, my head no clearer, my lungs clogged with the humid air.

"Ready?" I nod, the two of us riding side by side, we followed the sat-nav along a different route, until we turned onto Bluff Road once again.

Jess

The door explodes open, Ron walks in his tee shirt clinging to him, the demon who I now know as Hank, is quick to react, pushing Ron back out of the room "Tabitha said to wait." He states calmly.

"I'm done waiting, get out of my way" Ron demands and then I feel him pull energy from me, as he pushes the Demon out of his way. The demon takes flight, landing against the opposite wall.

A second whoosh of movement and the old Vampire has Ron, his hand wrapped around the back of his neck "Out!" comes his loud bark "Now!" a second command. I find myself wanting to comply. Swinging my legs out from under the covers, like a puppet on strings.

"Stay Witch!" I freeze, feet dangling over the edge of the mattress.

I watch the Vampire drag Ron from the room. Hank closes the door behind them and whatever spell I'd been under audibly pops.

Hank comes over, gently tucking me back into bed. "It's too soon, did he hurt you?" he asked with genuine concern written over his human features.

Exhaustion takes my words, slipping into sleep, I follow Ron outside the room dreamily, he's sitting on the sofa under the window again. The vampire king berating him about his place and patience. Demanding his obedience with the current situation. I bring sleep to us both, pulling gently at the serpents that bind us, I pull back the power that remains within them. I don't know yet, if Ron knows what he's done, I feel the adrenaline of my power coursing through our connection.

As sleep buries itself into me, an old vision replaces reality, I'm standing in a small one room building, it's little more than a brick hut, peering out the window like gap in the stonework, I watched not for the first time, as hundreds of people walked five or six deep along the dirt path towards the bridge. It's an Indian

festival, they are on route to temple, any moment now and panic will spur this crowd to trample so many underfoot as misinformation spreads. And then its blank and I don't recall the next scene.

When I wake it's dark outside, I know Hank is back in his corner, although I can't see or even hear him, if he is breathing, he's silent while doing it. It is his odor that alerts me of his presence.

"You good?" he inquires moments later, obviously knowing I'm once again awake. Taking measure of myself "I'm fine, but I need the restroom." I reply groggy from sleep.

A second later Hank gently helps me to my feet, his arm held aloft as aid, he steadies me, together we take the few feet to the en suite. Planting me safely on the commode he helps, not for the first time, in the removal of my lower garments, before leaving the room and gently closing the door behind him.

I know he's listening, but at least the door is closed, I do my business, standing on weak legs, I make it to the sink without assistance to wash my hands. Hank hands me a towel to dry them on. I heard him reenter the room, as I turned on the facet, I know he's trying to help. Taking the towel without comment, I make quick work of drying my hands. Once again Hank guides me back to bed, with an arm braced to catch me should I fall.

"Jesus! Let me be" I shrug out of his light grasp "Stop hovering!"

"I do not hover!" Hank gathers me back into place, his hold determined not to allow a second escape, as we continue back to the bed.

"For fucks sake! I'm not broken!" I exclaim as he hoists me back onto the bed.

"You've been asleep for days, your mind may want to fight me, but be assured your body is not ready for that fight!" tucking my legs under the covers, he fluffs the pillow behind. "Now be a good little Witch and do as your told!"

My blood boils at his words, I'm anything but little and the last thing I need is a Demon who wants to play Daddy! "Get out!" I scream.

"Furthermore, it is I who gives commands and for you to obey. Do not try me Witch! For your bottom is ivory and delicate, you wouldn't want me to set if aflame now, would you?" His hand slips to the leather belt he is wearing in warning.

"Delicate? you need your eyesight checked, I'm far from delicate!"

"Witches that play with fire, tend to get burned and if you talk negatively about yourself again, I will prove my point." Pausing he pulls the belt loose from his pants "Hush little one or I'll tire you out!" he warns, setting the belt on the side table as a visual threat.

In reply, I turn over, curl up under the covers, having already experienced that kind of punishment at human hands, I have no desire to visit it under the hand of a Demon.

I heard him chuckle as he returns to his corner. Prick! I mouthed silently, before once again allowing sleep to take me.

Tank

My charge is entertaining with her combative words, I looked forward to the next time she is awake. Watching her form, curled under the covers, she seems to favor sleeping on her side, turning numerous times in any given hour. Her sleepy whimpers with the adjustments, enticing my manhood to hardened with desire.

I've walked this earthly plain a multitude of times, taken human females into my care. She is right, I enjoy taking care of the earthbound females. Their form appeals to me in ways other demons never could. With the right little girl, I enjoy the role of caretaker, setting rules, giving both pain and pleasure.

The first meal I fed Jess, she'd been so sweet, opening her mouth for each spoonful of soup I'd pre-cooled with my own breath. Neither of us spoke, no instruction necessary as she enjoyed the chicken noodle soup. I made care not to rush her, allowing her time not only to swallow, but to enjoy and gather strength from each mouthful. Her lips parting in a silent signal that she is ready for the next spoonful.

Having laid my belt beside her, promising pain for her combative attitude, I impatiently wait for her to wake, she is regaining herself and I know from her recent actions she will be ready to fight me, this next time she'd want to feed herself. Even though I know she not mine, my own desire has me planning to take charge of the little human witch, sleeping before me. I envision myself forcing the point.

She turned from right to left side once more, but her heartbeat gives her away, she is awake. My dick jumps in anticipation "Hi, sleepy head."

She lets out a sigh, as she rights herself. Stepping over quickly, I assist her, standing her pillow long-ways to give support.

"Stop!" she complains as she tries to pull the pillow out of my grasp.

"Feeling better, does not allow for bad manners, little Witch." I warn.

"Move!" she instructs as she makes to extract herself from the bed.

"Where are we going?" I ask, without backing up or giving her space to dismount the higher-than-normal mattress, which allows for under bed storage.

"We. Aren't. Going. Anywhere!" She punctuates each word as she shuffles getting ready to dismount the bed.

I scooped her into my arms "Now where to?"

"Put me down!" she struggles for escape.

"I don't think so. Now for the last time, where are we going little one?"

"Hell, if I know, put me down!" she hollers

"Hell? Well, if you insist."

"What?! No! Put me down!"

"You sure? I have a rather cozy spot down there, it's not all flames and gore in Hell you know, wouldn't take but a sec to get there?" I tease.

"NO!" Her screech, full of desperation this time, has me placing her back on the bed.

"Only joking, little one." I chuckle, pulling the covers up over her bent legs as she tucks them in on herself. I place a butterfly kiss on her forehead.

"Yuck! Get off me!"

"You don't find my form handsome? I'm deeply hurt."

"Demon, you smell."

I made a show of sniffing my armpits to her disgust. "You may have a point, after dinner we will shower."

Just then one of the locals comes in with her nightly meal. As I'd instructed it's my favorite dish, tomato soup. Taking the bowl from the guy. She's shifts under the covers, scooting towards the center of the queen-sized bed.

"I got it." Reaching out for the bowl in my hand.

Setting the bowl on the small table, I turn to face her "Are we to fight about this now too?" "No, hand me the soup, I can feed myself." She directs.

"For the past ten nights, I've sat here and taken good care of you, have I not?"

"Yes, and now I can do it myself, so thank you, but I got it from here." She decrees.

Flipping her over, pinning her legs straight, beneath me, I pulled her shirt up, her plump bottom covered only in her knickers, I catch her wrists, gathering them into one hand, I placed them in the center of her back. Effectively holding her place. My other hand giving her rear a dozen, flicks with my palm.

Having taken her off guard I get those first licks in without verbal response. She lies frozen in place, her lack of further struggle unexpected. Taking the opportunity to warm her rear some more, this time I laid more weight behind the slaps.

She remains silent, void of any response. Having never spanked a Witch before, I reach over and scooping the belt into my hand. Laying a handful of strips across her blooming arse. Still no reaction.

Releasing her hands, she relaxes them into the very spot I'd placed them. Puzzled, I flip her back over, not a single tear has fallen, she gives no outward sign she'd even taken the strips I'd laid without restraint. I searched her for some kind of acknowledgment, any kind of reaction. But she's gone mute and remains motionless.

Extricating myself from the bed, thinking she'd make a comment with some distance between us, but she remains unmoving.

"Say something." I order as I grow impatient with concern, she is still physically and mentally weak from the events of so many days ago?

I feel the energy crackle in the room around me. She springs from the bed, rage painted clearly in place, across her angel features. "How dare you!" The air becomes solid, realizing too late, she wraps me in a bubble, not unlike the one she encased Christopher in just days ago.

"Ron! This Demon took what is yours!" she bellows, as I struggle to pull air into my current forms lungs. Francis blinks into being behind her, but her shields prevent even him from getting within arm's reach.

Ron follows him into the room, moments later "Jess? Release him!" he demands.

And just like that I pull air into my lungs, the bubble gone, I watch in amazement as Jessica, my little witch brushes past Francis and into Ron's waiting embrace.

"I need space." I heard her whisper into his chest.

Ron

Jess collapsed into my embrace, she'd asked for space and promptly fainted, holding her limp body in my embrace. Hank struggles with breathing over in the corner, while Francis spins on us.

"What was that?" Francis demands of me.

"It…It…it was me." Tank stutters over several gulps of air "I took liberties that weren't mine to take" he continues. "Francis, I should take my leave of this situation and return home."

"She's passed out?" Francis questions, disregarding Tank's request.

Scooping her into my arms "Explain, Tank?" Stepping towards the bed, I placed her back into it. Pulling the covers across her lightly I noticed the belt that lies on the side table.

"You whipped her?" I spin on the demon king.

"I did" he's unapologetic.

"Why?"

"I became enthralled with her, it was my mistake, it'll be best for me to return home." "Yes!" Francis agrees, excusing the demon from this realm.

"I think I have proved that I can indeed control her power, it's time for her and me to move towards the next stage." I pressed Francis for his agreement.

"Be careful guardian, be very careful with your charge." He blinks out of existence on the heels of Hank's own disappearing act.

Only the shifter, Baron remains in the safe house. He's not left his room to investigate the commotion.

Closing the bedroom door, I gently lay beside her, nonchalantly brushing her hair from her face. Watching her sleep, her breathing steadily, I prop my head up on the crook of my arm.

Jess

Waking up, his arm lies heavily around my middle. Shifting carefully away, he pulls me in closer than before. The gentle rumble of his snoring telling me he was unaware of this action. My stomach rumbles with hunger and my bladder tells me that it needs attention as well.

I replay the events of earlier, the rage had been blinding as I encased that demon in my bubble, whatever the connection between Ron and I, it is very different to the one I'd grown into adulthood with. Never could I communicate in my dreams with Christopher, and now I'm lying in Ron's embrace, the power dancing between us. It is intoxicating!

"Yum! Yes! You are that!" sleepy words from Ron lips seem to agree.

Has he risen from his slumber? The next rumble of his rhythmic snoring answers my unspoken question. My stomach and bladder complain in unison "Ron?"

In response he gathers me even closer, tucking my head under his chin, my arms squeezed between us in an uncomfortable position.

Exasperated with his tight embrace, I push hard into him, trying to get my arms free "RON!" I complained "Let me go!" I demand, shoving against his solid chest "Ron! Wake. Up!" I press.

"Quit struggling, Princess."

"Get off me!" I demand.

"But you're so perfect" he whines "So comfortable and cozy, I'm never gonna let you go again." "Fuck you! Get off!" I shoved again "I need to pee, stop playing, let me up, for fucks sake, Ron?" He chuckles in reply, his hold like a vice, not giving me an inch "Does my Princess need a piss?" he toys.

"Fuck you!"

"Yes Please"

"Ron, come on I'm not joking, you want me to piss the bed?"

"Not my bed" he laughs.

Sending an ether shock into him, exasperated with his current game, as I struggle against him.

"Mm, tickles" his hand moves, giving me a moment's thought that I'd finally gotten through to him, instead he anchor's me in place with his heavy leg, and starts to tickle my exposed side.

He knows I am extremely ticklish, twisting in vain to extricate myself from his hold, but it's useless as he continues tingling. My giggling has my bladder releasing "Stop!" I beg between giggles "Shit!"

"Princess? Why is my leg wet?"

"Stop!" I beg, through breathless giggles.

"Fine! Go! Abandon my embrace if you must?"

"Fucker!" I squealed in his direction, as I scoot quickly off the bed. Standing, my legs threaten to give way, wet from my belly down, thanks to his ticklish onslaught. My bladder more than halfway empty at this point.

"Language Princess" his words caution as I scurry into the en suite, turning to close the door, I stick my tongue out at him before quickly lashing the door closed between us.

Taking the advantage of having him locked out of the en suite, I turn the shower on, setting it to steamy temperature, I finally take time to wash the past several days off my tired body. The odor of urine and Demon insulting my nose, now replaced with Irish spring body wash.

Facing the shower head, I relax in the water, not hearing Ron enter the room, he surprises me with a slap to my still tender rear. "Now that wasn't very nice" he comments as his fingers traced the lines made by the demon's belt earlier.

"No, can't say I enjoyed it."

"Wasn't talking about the whipping Princess. Little girls that stick their tongues out, generally taste soap."

"Oh! Don't you start!" exasperated with his words, I reach for the shampoo, and begin the process of taking care of my long hair, not caring if soap falls into his face behind me.

"Hands, on the wall Princess, legs wide"

Spinning to face him, I tried to push him out of the shower "I asked for space?!" He twirls his finger in front of me in silent instruction.

"I have soap in my hair!"

"Yes, yes you do, turn assume the position, Princess."

Standing here soaking wet, I know sending any static electricity would only attack us both, and last time he'd taken a powerful charge like it was nothing, so I huffed "Fine!" whipping my hair around, hoping that my soap ladened hair would reach my intended target.

"Now that wasn't very nice" he comments as he closes what little distance remains between us "And I was going to be so very kind, before you got soap in my eye" his hand reaches between my legs, his fingers spreading my labia, before two fingers invaded me fully without preamble.

He strokes me roughly, increasing his invasion quickly to three fingers, and then four. Continuing his onslaught, disregarding my calls for him to stop.

Then I'm empty, he thumbs my most precious

of buttons, and then nothing, he's edging me repeatedly, his hand takes me again, only to leave me
hanging on the edge, my calls for him to stop, soon
changing to begging "Please!"

"Princess, what do bad girls get?" He continues to
tease me, I'm so very close, and again he pauses. The
emptiness driving me mad with need, his onslaught
keeping me so close, building the need to painful
desertion.

"Princess, I'm waiting?"

I can't think, his torture voiding everything else
into nothingness. Tears fall freely as frustration
over his endless torture overtakes me. Again,
he pauses, my legs trembling, barely holding me
upright. I know this game, although we'd never
done it in a shower before, his sharp smack to my
tender buttocks, giving another point to focus on.

"Tell me Princess, what happens to bad little
girls?" His thumb squeezes my over sensitive button
painfully one more time.

"Pun... p... punishment!"

"Yes, punishment." He confirms as he once again
leaves me void of his touch, holding my sides he
changes his position "turn around and drop to your
knees."

I know he's seen what this does to me, he's seen
my memories, I turn, tears flowing, I know better
than to deny him, I'll get this done, I'll take him and

expertly, I'll bring him to his own explosive orgasm, with eyes raised so he can watch as I swallowed everything he has to give.

His hands take my head as expected, but they are moving unexpectedly, confusion consumes me. He's washing my hair, removing the shampoo, gently? Ensuring none of the soap washes forward into my eyes.

"There's my good girl, Princess you finish showering, I'll get us both towels" with that he exits the shower, leaving me wanting and totally confused.

Ron

I gave the familiar order for her to face me, hearing her determined promise to finish me quickly unexpectedly via connection. Her inner dialog as she prepares herself mentally, the emotions flowing like a storm through me. Disgust! Pain and sorrow, it melts my intention, as I reached for her head, as I've had million times before, I pause, unable to force her into the intended action, I do the only thing left to do, I used the stream of water coming down upon her to wash out the shampoo still remaining in her hair.

Her emotions becoming my own, I finished the task gently, my own need vanishing, my own voice full of self-disgust. Stepping out, I gather a towel around myself, pausing before leaving the en suite to lay out two towels and a clean nightie before leaving her alone.

Toweling myself dry, putting my jeans back on, I shake her emotions free as I leave the room. She's not the only one of us that needs space, even with the Kings gone this bungalow is still brimming with the local club members. I motion for one of the locals to guard her bedroom door as I head for the front door.

When her mobile phone registers an incoming message, given the sound it made, I know it's yet again her daughter trying to videochat. Looking at the open app, she's already tried four times in the last few hours to make contact.

Resigned to her daughter's persistence, I about turn, going back into the room I'd just vacated. Jessica is reentering the bedroom as I enter.

"You'll need to read the conversation I've been having with your youngest." I toss the mobile phone towards her.

Anger blazes in her eyes, but she caught the phone and begins thumbing up through the message screen.

"Before you call her back, you need to promise to stick to the story."

Taking a seat on the edge of the bed, she glares coldly at me, then rereads the message thread. Moments become minutes, her anger hot when I'd first given her phone back, seems to cool as she rereads the messages. Then her rage hits me full force once again, I don't think she is aware I can feel her emotions.

Her fingers tremble, she cuts me a look, then I see

her swipe the screen left, I continue to watch her closely as she opens a different app "Am I supposed to be thankful?" The sting in her voice cracks slightly.

"You're on a training course."

"Yes, I see that! And now you expect to lie?"

"Your youngest is very stubborn, not unlike her mother, you should call." I take a seat at the bottom of the bed. I watch as Jess thumbs back and forth over the screen. Her emotions are raw, painful, she's not impressed with the lies I've told, but as time moves on, she settles into resignation of the task at hand. I'm aware that she's extremely annoyed with my continued presence. But I see it as a necessary evil, she's not ready to surrender to my guardianship, the kings are finally gone, leaving me to move toward the next stage in their plan.

The phone alerts again to an incoming videochat request, not being able to see the screen myself, I know from her reaction who it is. Nodding I give silent permission for her to answer.

"Hey" Jess answers as she turns to sit with her back against the bed headboard. Hers knees up, to block me from her view "What's up?" she asks, only a slight tightness in her voice.

"I just wanted to chat" her daughter comments "How's it going?"

"Not much down time, its rather boring to be

honest. Seems we're getting a completely new system, I've been picked to train our department and then I'll go on to teach throughout the company, I'm probably gonna be busy for the foreseeable future." Jess relaxes into the lie, and even gives us an open ended extension on her abscess.

Satisfied with her mother's statement, they move onto the mundane of regular life. Jess becomes comfortable with the conversation, but I refuse to leave her alone. It's all just a little too easy for the Jessica I know. I have my own cell recording the conversation, so I can replay it and make sure that she doesn't say anything to make her daughter think anything is wrong. They talk for well over two hours, then finally Jess makes her excuses with talk of being tired and yawns to match, before finally hanging up the conversation.

Then she flips to another app on her phone and brings it to her ear, 'Speaker' I mouthed.

Exasperation peels across her face, but she does as I ask without comment "Hey!" Laughter follows "Oops! You're in the bathroom?"

"I am" he chuckles.

"Just called to say I'm still in the land of the living" She responds with a laugh in her voice. "About time!" He seems annoyed.

"Schedule here is something else, I'll call back if you like."

"Sounds good, love you."

"You're mad!" she replies and then hits the end button. Offering the mobile phone to me. When I don't reach out fast enough, the phone slips from her hand to the mattress between us.

Jess

G rateful my timing with the call to my husband was one of tradition, I allowed the phone to fall to the mattress, I wasn't stupid enough to think he'd let me keep it.

Making light work of getting up and crossing over to the bedroom door, pulling it open, I'm not surprised to find a young biker on the other side. "Move!" I challenge pushing past him.

He's slow to react and complains as energy passes between us "Next time, I won't ask" I comment without apologizing.

"Play nice!" comes Ron command from behind me, as I continue down the hallway. The guys in the hallway are jumping out of my way quickly as I near the end of the hallway. I'm not running, in truth I've no idea where I'm going or what I'm planning, I just need to get out of that room.

"Stop!"

The command peals through me, rooting in place, mid step. Spinning around on him, I pull on my power, allowing the rage to build and take over. I pull through the lengths of the serpents that bind us and I envision dragging him to his knees.

"Jessica! STOP!"

Ron remains standing, I pull on the energy again.

"Place!" comes his next word, complete with finger motion "Down, Jessica" he punctuates the fingers motion.

My knees crumple beneath me, he's pulling back the energy I've stolen and compelling me to follow his direction. I feel pain in my wrists, unlike the flames of his brother, this is deep pressure like that of a bite.

Taking a step back, I grab hold of the closet thing near me, its turns out to be a pants leg, I used it to prevent my descent as I attempt to bring the energy back to me.

Gathering my strength, I'm able to right myself, I release my hold on the person beside me and yank more of the energy my way. The pain from the bites eases as the power swings my way "How dare you!" I bellow "You dare to control me." I grind out as I force him to his knees.

The energy see-saws between us, neither of us doing more than standing on trembling limbs, the initial shock of his first attempt of control wearing off, the onlookers frozen in our unseen struggle.

"Witch, yield!" Ron cries painfully as the struggle

continues.

In truth I can win this battle anytime now, his control over the serpents while painful, are no match to my true power, but I'm coming to my senses, surprise of his attack gone, I realize how dangerous it would be with so many witnesses for me to win this battle of wills so easily.

I begin to make a show of weakening against him, until finally I allow the energy to pop between us and I go down onto my knees, I settle in fake exhaustion with my forehead bowed forward on the floor in front of where I sit. Holding my wrists in my lap as the pressure he has supplied down our connection has increased as I given into his control of the energy we share.

"Leave us" Ron's own exhaustion of the unseen exchange plain in his voice.

Ron

The hallway empties in no time. I'm exhausted, the Kings had explained how the chains worked, but the serpents are an unknown; thankfully I can still feel the power flow between us. Jessica has settled into her position of full submission, although I'm not convinced by her display of surrender. With the witnesses gone, I ready myself for her temper.

"Guardian?"

Her voice is toneless, just an open-ended statement without request. I don't respond, the need for complete privacy from prying ears foremost on my mind. "Terry?" I call, knowing he is listening from the kitchen.

"Yes Guv" he replies popping his head into the hallway from the opening.

"Empty the house, everyone outside, and Terry?"
"Yes?"

"I do mean everyone, text me when it's done." I instruct.

"Gotcha!"

I go into the front room, grab one of the cheap plastic chairs into the hallway, placing it in front of Jessica. Taking a seat, placing one leg comfortably across the other, I lean it back into the wall behind me. The only noise is our mutual rhythmic breathing.

I search out our connection now that I've recovered somewhat, the energy between us is balanced once more. The text message pings its alert on my mobile phone, a quick glance confirms it's from Terry.

"You can quit pretending now." I say coldly, as I watch Jessica both through our connection and visually.

Sitting back on her hunches, she gives me a death glare "You can release your vangs now, you won!" she spits out as she does.

Looking past the glare, I slowly drop my gaze over her chest and to her lap, where she is rubbing both wrists.

"Huh?"

"Stop biting me through our connection, please."

I reach further along our connection and visualizing the serpent's I see the fangs are sunk deep into her wrists. I pull back and watch as the serpents slowly retreat, then finally wrap themselves around her wrist, the heads settle along the back of her hands.

Allowing reality to form once more around me, I take note that Jess has stopped holding her wrists now "Oops!" I grin with satisfaction of my ability "can we call a truce?"

I feel her temper rise at my words "A truce? Seriously? Fine! You win! Can I go home now?" but her voice is coated in boredom.

"I think we both know, I didn't win" I challenge "you gave me the win. And no, you cannot go home... not yet anyway, you have work to do."

"Work?"

"Yes, but first let's settle this."

"You won already!"

"Did I?" I shake my head at her obvious lie "We'll see how true that is shall we?" I will assess her resolve the old-fashioned way "In there, strip, in place with that Demons belt in your hands, you remember how?" I instruct.

"I remember" she replies, her eyes blazing with fury.

"What are you waiting for? That's additional ten for making me wait."

Watching her stiff movements as she rises, I almost reach out to assist her. It makes me wonder if she really is exhausted. I'll give her time to get into position, satisfied that she has resolved herself to complying, as she's reentered the bedroom without further comment, I head into the kitchen.

Checking the cupboards, I locate the olive oil and from the refrigerator, I discover a good-sized piece of fresh ginger root. I take out a small metal spoon and use it to peel the ginger. Finally, I gather a glass of ice and I head for the bedroom.

Pausing in the doorway, I take in the sight before me, Jessica's arms are slightly bent behind her, the belt held below her buttocks, her head settled to one side as she bends over the side of the mattress. Due to the height of the bed, she's on her tippy toes, so her middle crests the mattress.

I drag my chair from the hallway into the room, placing the items I collected from the kitchen onto the seat, I step up behind her, running my fingers over her exposed rear.

"Spread those feet." I tap her bottom.

I trail a finger along the length of her spine, slowly down and into her crack. She stiffens as I circle her anus before retracing my path back up her spine. I enjoy the shiver of her muscles as they react to my tender touch. Placing one firm smack to her rear as I finish my tortuous path, and then ten more in rapid fire, alternating sides, to paint her bottom a pretty, pink evenly. These don't count, they are just warm ups, I know she recalls the structure for this kind of thing.

Taking a moment to admire the warm ups design,

adjusting my position so she can see me "Tell me Princess, how many do think is suitable for your transgressions of recent?" I know she hates this part,

more than the whipping itself, which is of course why I do it. Whatever the number she comes up, is just a starting point. Too low and I'll quadruple it.

"The Demon has already marked me." She remarks in a hopeful reminder "and you already plan on an additional ten for my delayed response."

"I am aware, the Demon had no place touching you, but none the, less it has happened, neither of us can do anything about that now, and what are his are not mine. So?" The reminder of the Demons actions only add fuel to my annoyance.

"I'd like to also remind you; it has been quite a long time since I've endured such punishments."

"And yet, here we are? The next thing out of that devilish mouth better be a number or you'll forfeit, you do remember the automatic solution to that?" The dealers' choice was evil, and I would enjoy every moment of it.

"Forty?"

"Are you asking me or telling me?"

"Telling." Although there was still a thread of uncertainty in her voice.

"Fifty, including the extra ten. Sounds fair for the attempted escape today." I agree. "What? I wasn't running! I was…"

"Was what? You left the room without permission, pushed past the door guard, shocked at least six more members as you went down the hallway and then you fought me for power! You know, I think dealers' choice works better, come to think of it!"

"Fuck you!" She spits, dropping the belt, rising from her position. I place a hand in the center of her back, pressing her back down firmly.

"Do I need to bind you in place?" I ask as she settles back down. I scoop the belt up from the floor, giving a couple of light taps with the folded belt in silent request for her open her closed fists. Placing the belt back in its previous place. "Well?"

"No, Guardian."

Sitting with my arm across her middle, I warmed her bottom with several even smacks of my bare hand. Jessica remains motionless. "Spread those feet, Princess." In the shuffle of placement, she'd allowed them to gather once more. Once she's adjusted, I lay ten more rapid fire smacks across her warming rear. "We are agreed then, dealer's choice?"

"Agreed."

Laying a few more light taps, she's aware that her answer is missing the final number, so I continue to tap and wait for her to adjust her answer.

"Dealer's choice, Guardian." She finally acknowledges.

Standing, I retrieve the olive oil and ginger, I pour the oil along her crack, allowing it to run down and over her anus, she inhales at the sensation of my finger massaging some around her entrance. I use the oil to lubricate the ginger root as well, I work my thumb into her exit. Once I'm happy with the condition of her sweet spot, I begin to press the ginger into her anus.

"Relax" I coax her gently, as I apply further pressure, until it slips into place, a good thick inch piece is snugly in place. "Good girl." I praise, knowing that the ginger has only just begun to mix with her juicy anus.

Standing I retrieve a cube of ice from the waiting glass, I trail it over her warm butt, allowing it drip down towards the ginger, knowing that it will add to the gingers burn.

I leave it sitting at the top of her crack and reach for a second piece of ice. This one I insert without preamble into her vaginal slit. I hear her hiss and can't help but tease "Yes Princess?" I asked with no real expectation of an answer.

Wasting no further energy on setup, removing the belt from her grasp. The first strike has the ice on her bottom, falling off. Its purpose fulfilled I don't stop, as I continue to crisscross her bottom "Count?" I do not pause, she's a smart witch and has been keeping count, starting her verbal count as twelve, which sounds about right.

I break after the twenty-fifth strike, place my palm gently to her rear, I evaluate the temperature of her skin, making sure that while I am marking her, I'm not causing her permanent damage. I pull the ginger out a little then reseat it, chuckling as Jess emits another satisfying hiss. Some of the ice has melted in the glass, with fingers splayed over the top of the glass I pour the liquid along her spin. The cold

produces another hiss.

Stepping back into a new swinging position, I begin again, setting a new set of lines across her already tender behind. Her counting starts without reminder this time. I know she had suggested forty, but now as we reach the number, I pause. She's not foolish enough to believe we are finished. Afterall she still had the additional ten she earned for her delayed response, but with it now being dealer's choice, I admire my work so far, check again the condition of her skin. It's hot and welted, but intact, setting my mind to the task once more, I lower my strikes now, catching the tender thigh and under bottom section. We've superseded fifty now, and I still see room for improvement.

Pausing at sixty, I once more check her skins temperature, I squeeze her tender mounds, which grants me another hiss. "You, okay?" I ask checking her temperament.

"Fuck you!"

"Another fifty it is then."

"No! Please no! Guardian, I'm Ow! Um? Sixty-one!"

I place a mix of light and hard lashes up and down her already tender area. Her counting is an assortment of numbers and pleads. She cries out at seventy-five and I can see she is coming apart. Pausing I pull the ginger free; this brings new tears as the air only serves to reheat the inner entrance of anal opening. I lay a further five to her thighs, I hear audible relief as the belt hits the floor.

Stooping down behind her, I massage the stiffness in her legs, working my way up to her tender bottom, I stand up behind her. I run my fingers between her never region, I play with her clit, dipping my fingers into her vaginal opening, I stretch it, sweeping her juices towards her anal opening, her juices mix with the reminder of the ginger and the hiss I receive confirms I've reheated that area.

Freeing my rock-hard cock from its confines, I place it at her hot exit, and push, taking it slowly, my fingers encourage from underneath, she's so moist, I can sense her orgasm building, I'm fully seated in her anal passage now.

She's weeping quietly, it's a mix of emotions, pain and pleasure, as I begin to pull out, I rock slowly back and forth, building my own need to explode. The remnants of the ginger juice, heating my passage, I increase my pace as my explosion overtakes the need to torture her further.

I come hard and fast, holding her underneath, as her own explosion, pulls me in further as she squeezes down, her empty vagina void of completion.

Pulling out, I give her one more hard slap on her rear "Go get cleaned up!"

Jess

Taking in my reflection in the large en suite mirror, dark circles, and familiar tired eyes stare back at me. The sting in my rear is nothing compared to the need between my legs. Turning around slightly, I can see the welts left by the Demons belt. I dare to place my own fingers across them, the burning so recognizable, memories of past times, flip like the pages of a book through my mind. I wonder how long he'll force me to wear his reminder this time. My legs still wear patterns that I was unable to repair given the length of time Christopher had made me wait to heal myself.

This body a mixed reminder of old and new scars, I long stopped caring for my own well being, hiding in plain sight, but in a body of my own neglect. My latest visit to the doctor I'd been told of yet another organ declining, this bodies medical condition an ever growing list of labels and error codes.

I used the hand towel to wash away the tears from my face, a face I hate, looking at the person that reflects at me, I looked so much like my mother, a woman that I could never please, a woman that was jealous of my connection with my father, a man she claimed to love. My father's love for her was endless but she never seemed to reciprocate it. Then again you never know how things are behind closed doors, there had to be something.

Stepping back into the bedroom, I don't bother with clothing, getting back under the covers, everything hurts and not just his welts. I leave those exposed as I snuggle the covers under my chin. Closing my eyes, listening pass the open door, the sounds of cooking and smell of coffee have my stomach growling, it's been a while since my last meal.

Ron enters the room after what seems like forever, I open my eyes to see him setting a plate and mug on the table next to the bed.

"You should eat" it's not a command and I certainly don't disagree, but I'm in no hurry for him to see me struggle into a seated position. He runs a hand over my tender bottom "Pretty" he comments.

So much for hoping he'd allow me to heal anytime soon. Closing my eyes once more, I block him out of my mind, and try to think of something other than the heat coming from my rear and thighs.

I feel the weight of him as he joins me in bed, his hand gathering my hair behind me, I don't have any strength left to complain, his fingers run down my side and over to my belly. His hand wonders downwards, but stops just shy of my curly haired mound, as another growl comes from my tummy.

"Jessica?"

"Guardian?" I groan, wishing he'd just let me be for a while. His hand makes its way up to cup a breast "while this body isn't unenjoyable, I think it's time to fix it."

I start to pull on the ether around us, gathering in healing energy, unsure just how much I'll be able to repair, removing his recent punishment would be easy, but getting this tired body into working order, would take more time.

The sensation in my rear dissipates easily as I repair my outward appearance, the folds I've become well associated with over the years, curl inwards, as the skin becomes tight around the areas where the fat melts away.

My nipples perk upwards as the breasts become more taught, the flab on the back of my arms dissolves, I pour the energy into my outward appearance, things long ignored gather and slowly my form takes on that of a person that has exercised enough to keep smooth curves and sculpted muscles.

Inwardly, I feel some improvement but I'm fully aware that the autoimmune issues I have won't be fixable. I'm diabetic and have issues with most of my major organs.

"That's better" Ron comments as he explores my improved form, placing his hand where just moments ago, he'd whipped me "I have a clean canvas, don't give me reason to paint it again today" his tone is playful, but no less a warning that he might make me wear the next design much longer "time to eat." He reminds me with a gentle tap to my bottom, confirming his threat, before he releases me and gets off the bed himself.

I'm tempted to curl up under this cover and just sleep, but he's right, I do need to eat, so I adjust into a seated position, leaning against the headboard "Would you be so kind as to pass me a top of some kind?" I ask sweetly.

He takes his time admiring my new and improved chest, before stalking over to the dresser and grabbing the first thing his hand falls on. It a black tank top, passing it to me, I note the skull and roses design as I slip it over my head "Thanks".

"Don't linger in here too long, eat, drink and get dressed." He seems annoyed as he turns to leave.

He's always been moody, but now that he's not holding my attention, I realize the top he handed me smells of herb. Turning my attention to the mug, I take in a lungful of its dark aroma, it's not enough to expel the odor coming from the top, but it does help.

The ham omelet he plated has gone cold, but still with the help of the coffee, I manage to swallow it. Getting up I search for other clothing options, the clothes I'd come in are not here, the nightie he'd given me earlier and the clothes here all seem to be coated in the nasty musk of smoke and herb in the end, I put on a pair of men's joggers.

Venturing into the hallway, I note club members are starting to return, they give me a wide berth now as I walk towards the front of the house. I can hear Ron in the front room, it's a one-sided conversation, so I figure he's on the phone. Turning the corner, I see him passing back and forth, facing away from me, in

the middle of a heated conversation, he doesn't notice me enter the room. I prop myself on one of the stools that has been moved to the edge of the room. I always feel safer with a solid wall behind me.

"Tonight, at seven, fine!" Ron snaps to whoever is on the other end of the call "Yes! You don't need to tell me that!" He's furious "No…Right…Yup!" with that he's pushing the end symbol on the phone.

Turning he looks me up and down angrily "That's not going to work!"

I don't bother to respond, if he hates it that much, he can fix it, I simply shrug my shoulders.

"Marshall?" he hollers.

"Sir?" A dark skin kid pops his head into the room, his thin body glad, in dark jeans and a t-shirt. "Your girl outside? Have her come here a minute."

Marshall gives a quick nod before disappearing out of the room.

"I can smell you from here."

"And you think I can't?"

Just then Marshall reappears with his girl, a young thing by the looks of her.

"Find my Princess an outfit, something that doesn't smell of that crap! Marshall, you keep the girl's company and take Tank with you!" having given them his orders, Ron turns his attention to me "Behave!"

Shrugging my shoulders, I promised nothing. I follow the couple into the hallway, and out the front door.

"Shit!" I exclaimed as my bare feet connected with hot concrete. Marshall waves a hulk of a biker over, who immediately scoops me up and over his shoulder, fireman style.

"Hey!" I squealed with surprise, as the brute walks across the street and into the house directly opposite. He sets me down and holds on only long enough to let me regain my balance.

Following the young couple down the hallway and into a bedroom, which mimics the same size and setup of the one across the street.

"I'll be in the hallway Amber." Marshall kisses her on the forehead "don't hurt my baby girl." He requests of me as he leaves us alone, bringing the door closed behind him.

Taking in the room decor, it's obvious Amber and Marshall are into some kind of age play, an adult sized pacifier lies on the dresser, and a baby bottle sits next to it. Her pink paddle hanging above it. Amber stands nervously watching me, she holds her hands together in front of her nervously.

"I won't bite." Offering my hand in greeting "look I don't know how long I have, but I'd like to wash this stink off me, can you find me some things that might fit while I take a shower, if that's okay with you, that is?" I ask as kindly as I can muster.

"Um, Sure!" She replies, "Showers in there, I'll see what I can find." She sides steps my out reached hand and heads to her free-standing closet.

Dropping my hand, I head into her en suite, it's all too pink in here, fluffy bathmats, towels and shower curtain, even her hairbrush is pink. I shake my head, as I remove the top and joggers. Entering the shower, I apply her strawberry and cream bodywash to my body with my hands. I make light work of the shower, stepping out I wrap one of the towels around myself. "Do you mind if I borrow some of your perfume?" I call back into the bedroom.

"Help yourself Mame." I shake my head at the Mame comment and pick up the candy floss scented spray, lightly misting it across my arms.

Amber comes in with her arms full of hangers "My er Daddy won't let me wear these." She announces gingerly.

"Well then." I smile back "Let's see what will make mine mad." I grin.

"You're a little?" She questions.

"Used to be, now he's, my guardian." I take the top hanger from her, it's a plain black dress, the material is jersey and I know it'll be a hip hugger "What else you got there?"

I see her nervousness dissipate as we explore the outfits she's holding "Now we're talking I announce." As she holds up the next hanger of what must have been a dozen outfits "I can see why your Daddy won't let you wear that!"

She giggles "House wear only." She announces, looking over her shoulder she sticks her tongue out.

I join her in her giggles. "I think this is it, my new friend. Do you have any no-no undies, which would go dangerously with this?"

She holds up a finger, steps out of the en suite and I hear her pulling out the dresser drawer, she's back with me quickly. In her hands she holds up some barely their red lace panties and matching bra set.

"You sure I can have these; you might not get them back?" I ask genuinely.

She nods and hands them to me.

"Thanks Amber." Taking the undies, I make light work of dressing "How old is your little Amber?" I inquire as she helps me with the zipper on the skirt.

"Four, we should do your hair to match." She announces, no longer scared of the witch in her bedroom. I take a seat in front of her vanity, "I'm totally in your hands little one." I smile back at her.

She's already brushing my hair, and gathering ribbons, the red shiny ribbons she applies to my pigtails are perfect. The makeup she applies is flirty but not overdone, turns out she's going to school for Cosmetology.

Marshall knocks on the door thirty minutes later, "almost ready!" she calls in full little mode voice. "We need to find shoes, then we'll be out Daddy!"

"Make it quick, Amber" comes his deep Daddy voice.

"Yes Sir!" I reply for her, as she's already arse deep in a pile of shoes. She holds up a pair of lady Janes, I shake my head.

"Right!" She agrees and goes back to digging.

What I'd give for a selection like she has, then I see the red soles of a pair of heels "Would you part with those?" I ask unsure if I'm asking too much from her.

"Yes! Perfect!" She's giddy with excitement, as she passes the black patent, four-inch heels with bright red sole to me.

"You Sure?" I confirm, before accepting them and put them on.

"Do a twirl!" she stands back as I do as she's asked.

Grinning back at her I whisper, "out of ten, how mad do you think he's gonna be?" "Twelve!" she squeals "defiantly Twelve."

I nod "Ready?"

"You sure you want to do this?" She asks, concern stricken as the time to leave the room is upon us. I nod and gesture for her to lead the way.

Marshall's face tells me, he's onto our game straight away "Amber!"

"Don't punish her, it was my idea."

"And she knows what I think of that outfit." He turns his stern look on poor Amber, who has taken a step or two to hide behind me.

"So, now she can never disobey you again, cos I'm keeping the outfit." Taking Amber's hand, I walk us both past him, keeping her on my far side, so she can avoid his displeased hands. "Tank?" I nod, when we get to the front door.

Tank runs a hand through his hair, its accompanied with "Jesus!" as he opens the door and holds it open behind us as we pass. I walk head held high, as we cross the street and back up the path to the other house. I feel every eye between the houses on us, our escorts follow closely behind us. Giving Amber's hand one last squeeze, I pushed the door to the house open, making my way into the front room.

As expected, Ron is standing by the window, his arms crossed. Oh yeah! He watched us cross the short distance between houses. I strut to the middle of the room and do a twirl for added effect.

"Sorry Sir! I'll get her something else to wear. I'll be dealing with my girl tonight!" He's already about facing.

"Don't you dare!" I whirl on Marshall before his one step towards the door.

"She's on my list!" I announce returning my attention to Ron "On my list." I repeat for clarity.

"Marshall" Ron is amused by my protective state-ment "Witch is giving her immunity for this trans-gression; you will not punish her for this. And don't worry about the outfit. She'll regret her footwear soon enough."

Amber has remained at my side "What list?" she asks me quietly.

"It means little Amber has an older sister now." I tell her with a smile, "Your part of my family now, and I protect my family." I whisper back.

"My sister?"

"Yes! A witchy sister" I raise an eyebrow and grin

at her.

"When you girls are completely finished!" Marshall beckons Amber to his side. "You get a pass on the outfit but your rooms a mess, little girl!"

I give her a sisterly embrace, before turning her over to Marshall.

Ron

With Marshall and his girl gone, I have Jess give me a second twirl. "We've got a few hours before we have to leave." I gather Jess into my embrace, my hands find the bottom edge of the barely-there skirt "Pigtails are cute too!" I'm going to enjoy torturing her for this. "I hope those shoes are comfortable, cos you're not allowed to remove them until I tell you."

"It's a brand-new body."

"I can see that!"

"Does my guardian not enjoy what he sees?" she teases.

"Oh, I like it! You're gonna be cold when we hit the tarmac back home." I announce truthfully, while running a hand under the lacy crop top to pinch a nipple. "You may have saved little Amber's butt, but yours is all mine!" I squeeze one buttock with my other hand.

"Your punishment will have to wait; you've got some studying to do." I take her by the hand over to the couch, "Sit." Reaching over her, I retrieved the envelope from the windowsill. "Here read this!"

Jess takes the envelope, her whole demeanor altering with my change of mood, she opens it in silence, the first page is a color picture of the lacy we will be tracking starting tomorrow. The next page has the girl's details, name, date of birth, last known movements. The next has a photo of the suspected kidnapper, a vampire known as Rubec. The final item in the packet is a Ziploc bag holding a gold chain and blue ribbon.

"How long ago?" Jess is frowning.

"About six weeks. The kings were contacted when the werewolf's discovered vampires are involved."

"I'm not…" Jess paused her sentence unfinished. She was lost in the picture of the female vampire "I…" again her voice breaking this time. "She's not… " Jess stammers another incomplete thought.

Bending down in front of Jessica, I place gentle fingers under her chin, bringing her eyes away from the page and to meet my own "You're scaring me."

"Good!" Jess schools her face "She's not someone you want to meet!"

"You've met her before?"

"Yes! And I'd rather tango with the Kings, any other ghoul than be in a room with her!" Jessica slowly begins to shake her head no; my fingers having released their hold on her chin. "I'm no match for her. I'll do what I can to find the lacy but don't ask me to…"

Standing up abruptly, Jessica storms across the room "I'll not take her on!" she screams, as she continues out of the room.

"Stop!" I command.

"Fuck you!" I hear her respond and then the front door slaps shut in my face as I go to follow her.

Outside she's mounting one of the bikes "STOP!" I command again, this time I pull on the serpent's energy that links us.

Ignoring me, Jess kicks the bike off its stand and thrusts it into motion. The guys are running towards her, a couple try to grab the bike as she rides by. I scoop up a bike myself and take off in hot pursuit. Other bikes quickly follow suit. It's clear she has no idea where we are, as she makes a turn into a dead-end, with us on her tail. Jess spins the bike around, and is now headed into us, she's not slowing down either. I gestured for the guys to give her an opening, whatever has her running so scared, has her choosing to ride, which confirms she not thinking straight.

I turn and follow her, two more turns and she's found the open road, opening her ride up now, she's going over sixty miles per hour. She rides Bluff Road until it ends, then she turns right barely slowing, as the road begins to twist.

I catch up and ride up on her outside, I signal for her to slow down, she looks at me but ignores me. Pulling on our connection while riding down the road at any speed is beyond my newly learned skills, so I keep along riding along side.

The other guys keep pace a safe distance behind us, Jess seems to have a destination chosen now as she makes another turn. We're headed to the state park, I pull back a little knowing that she's calming down now and in control of herself again. Watching her ride with that tight skirt hitched up and her top hugging her, her hair sails behind either side of her head.

She's slowing down, of her own accord, as she realizes she's riding a motorbike. Her brake lights going on and off in rapid succession as she loses her nerve. Then she's on the grass verge, the bike on its side, her under it.

I pull to a controlled stop, prop my bike on its stand, cutting it off and dismounting. I walk over to where she laid down her ride, "You remember you don't know how, Princess?" I ask knowing only her pride is hurt.

"Help me!" She pleads pitifully.

The other guys have joined us now, they look at me, before lifting the bike off her. I offer a hand to help her back onto her feet.

Tank is examining his bike for damage, "What the

hell was that?"

"Princess can't ride" I explain teasing.

"Seemed to be doing just fine back there!" he exclaims "So what the fuck?"

"Princess?" I offer her the chance to explain. She's so damn cute when she puts her hands on her hips and pouts at me in reply. I take mercy on her, wrapping my arm around her, I pull her close to me, giving her rear a firm tap. "You'll ride home with me."

Tank mounts his own bike, while a couple of the other guys decide between them on how they are going to get the spare bike back to the house.

"Tank gets his payment for that stunt when we get back." I state as she wraps her arms around me, right before we head home.

Ron

By the time we reach the house, I feel like I have a vibrator wrapped around, every cell of her being is trembling.

Her shaking is so bad, Terry steps over quickly recognizing the situation "Come here" his voice tender, as he guides her from the back of my bike. Jessie has climbed onto his hip, like a small child does, her arms tight around his neck.

Dismounting myself, I see Tank making a beeline for young Jessie, he's furious as is his right, but I hold up my hand palm forward signaling for him to stop and stay back, turning my attention to young Jessie and poor Terry, who was currently having issues breathing, since Jessie is holding his neck so tight.

Stepping closer to them, I uncurled one of her hands from his neck, transferring it to the back of my neck "come to Daddy" I coaxed gently, Jessie shakes her head, replacing her hand back around Terry, her head tucked into his neck, as she tries to hide away from me.

Rubbing her back and shoulders gently, she tries to climb away from my touch, I send a silent curse towards my dead brother.

"Jessie, baby" I try "Look at Daddy, sweat heart?" I continued to rub and touch her back and shoulders "Let Daddy see your sweat face, baby" as she turns her head slightly towards me, I reached up to caress the side of her. "Come to Daddy baby" I coaxed.

Jessie still trembles from head to toe, as she continues to cling to Terry, supporting her grown weight with both hands, his feet planted firmly beneath them, he whispers for her to go to me. Watching them, reminds me of the past. Terry could give something I was never able to provide, emotional security!

"Jessie" I tenderly encouraged, my arms open for her to take "come to Daddy, baby girl."

Between my words and Terry's, after several long minutes, Jessie finally reaches out with one arm, to offer an exchange, I help her switch from Terry's hip to my front. Her arms wrapped behind my neck, and her head tugged under my chin, one of my hands under her and the other supporting her back.

I mouthed my thanks to Terry, who returns a nod of thanks, stepping aside, allowing us a clear passage up to the front door of the house.

As I walk, I feel her shift, her trembling ceases, and her body tensing, little Jessie is gone by the time I enter the front room of the house. I let Jessica down gently, allowing her time to adjust herself, I wait for her to lead our next interaction.

Having been so young, when my brother forced himself on her and took the chains the way he had, had left Jessica with multi-personalities, who it would be that stepped forward after her little was out in the open is a game of Russian roulette.

I watch as Jessica steps over to the envelope I'd handed her earlier, she picks up the Ziploc bag, flipping it over in her hands. "She's hurting, it's dark, cold!" her voice distance.

"Princess?"

"Yeah?" turning her eyes from the bag, tears falling slightly down her face "Rubec has her." "We thought that might be the case." Stepping towards her, Jessica takes a step backwards. "Oh Fuck! Where's the bike I took?"

"Outside, you'll need to talk to Tank about that" I say, reaching to snag my Witch to me, rubbing the tears away with my thumbs "You didn't do much more than scratch it." I explain, knowing that the details will be fuzzy.

"I don't even remember getting on it!" she shakes her head "Fuck!" she exclaims again "Where is he?"

Taking her hand, I lead her back outside, Terry's

face is one big question mark of concern. Tank is right beside him "I filled him in Guv."

Letting go off my hand, Jess walks up to them "Tel?" she nods. Turning her attention to the large boulder of a man known as Tank "I'm sorry Sir, I offer myself for your judgment." Her voice clear and committed to her surrender.

Tank

T erry has told me how her mind and body are split, she's not crazy, it's the result of years of being twisted inside out by things she was too young to comprehend, but still the club rules are clear. Heck every biker knows not to touch another rider's bike without permission, let alone steal it.

"Theft here is a felony darling." I tell her sternly. She lowers her eyes, I look behind to see nod "If you were mine, you'd not sit easy for a month!"

"Sounds fair to me." Ron agrees. Taking her hand, I lead her over to my bike "Lay over the seat." I order.

A couple of our guys hold the bike in place, as she adjusts herself over the seat, I walk around the other side, taking in the minor damage she caused when she dumped it down, on top of herself. Making a full circle, and without preamble I lay a dozen quick slaps to her mini skirt clad behind.

She doesn't make any kind of acknowledgment in response to punishment. Looking over to her

Guardian in silent question, I give her another volley over the last set. Still nothing. "Does she even feel that?"

He shrugs and motions for me to continue.

I repeat the action, this time, setting each one heavier than the previous smack. Without the aid of the guys holding the bike still, both the bike and her would have fallen over with thunder I was giving. Still not getting a reaction from her has my blood simmering. Looking at the group of girls on the other side of the bike, I searched out my sister "Go get my tools." I instruct.

Surprise at my request flickers over my sister's face, but she makes her way through the group of members gathered behind her.

The crowd murmurs in the background, as I stalk the Witch laying over my seat. She's motionless, now I'm not hitting her rear, her outward appearance gives no reaction to the beating I've already applied.

Candy makes her way back through the group, my old guitar case in her hand, she sets it on the ground in front of my waiting victim. Candy turns on her heels, she knows the contents of the case very well, and I'm not surprised to see her walk back out of the crowd.

Kneeling next to it, I open it just enough for the Witch and I to see the contents of the case, my fingers wrap around the cane. Allowing the lid to close on its own, I make sure she sees what I'm holding.

Walking behind her, I make a show of whipping it in the air, giving Ronald the opportunity to stop me. Ron motions for me to begin, so I swing, hitting the skirt evenly across the middle of both buttocks. Giving no pause, I lay several more, crisscrossing so as not break the unseen skin beneath the fabric. Still no reaction, not even a hiss. "What gives?" looking over at Ron puzzled.

"Jessica, what's the count?" Ron instructs.

"In total? Thirty-eight."

Ron walks over with that announcement and lifts her skirt "I find she gets more attentive when you settle lower." He runs his fingers over the lines I've laid. "And it's forty-four, by my count." He taps her lightly and gestures for me to resume as he steps back, giving me space.

Having not kept count myself, I was surprised to hear that Ronald had. I touch my intended target, the place where butt meets thighs, placing a few quick flicks to judge my angle, I pull back and lay a strip on target.

"Let's call it one" I announce.

"One sir." She announces, but it's totally void of emotion.

"One, I will not touch things that are not mine,

sir" Ron corrects her.

She repeats the sentence, before I begin tapping again, this time in a different location. It's not long before we fall into a pattern. I tap, then apply the cane, she increases the count by one and repeats the sentence.

At twenty-five, I've painted her with stripes from upper thighs to middle of her rear, the welts angry as my own temper defuses. She's like a machine, taking each as if it's the first, not hissing or moving, even her voice remains pain free. Not prepared to break the skin over a few minor scratches to the bike, I go to put my weapon of choice away.

"May I?" Ronald asks as I go to open the case, his hand outstretched.

"You don't feel it's enough?"

"Oh, its plenty, but she's removed her shoes."

With a shrug, I hand over my tool. Ron steps to the side and picks up the foot nearest to him "What did I tell you?"

"Not to remove them, until you gave permission."

"And why is that?"

"Cos I'm a tease." She offered in reply.

With that he instructs her not to move and begins tapping the base of her foot. "Flex it!" he instructs, and then he applies the cane as she does. "Other side, Princess." I watch as he repeats the punishment on the other side. "Put your shoes back on, Princess."

He commands as he passes the cane back to me with a nod and a grin.

"Terry, take her inside."

Jess

Standing back up, my feet hurting more than my arse, I straighten my skirt and walk with Terry back towards the safety of the house.

Turning into the front room, I ignore my escort, and head over to the documents I'd been handed over earlier. I shuffle them so the one of the lacy is on top, standing I reread the details, our stories are similar in nature, she's what the wolves refer to as feral, but like me she has a guardian although the wolves don't call him that, he's her alpha and mate. We've even lived in the same area but not in the same circles. I fold the pages and stuff the contents back into the envelope.

Glancing out the window, I see the crowd has thinned, a Tahoe has pulled up outside, I turn around to see Terry leaning against the door frame.

"You good?"

"Just peachy!" I reply sarcastically. "I'm going to the toilet." I add as I approach him. Terry steps a side giving space to exit the room without issue. I head in the bedroom, closing the door behind me. After managing to urinate without touching the toilet seat, I face plant on the bed, extending my hearing past the door. But I don't hear anything of importance.

Ron

It's not been more than ten minutes, but I find Jessica, lying face down asleep when I enter the room, she's been occupying the last two weeks. I wish I could let her get the rest she needs, but we have a flight leaving in an hour and must get a move on.

"Time to go Princess" I can't resist giving her hot exposed arse a tap as I wake her with my words.

She rolls over, and quickly regrets it, flipping back onto her tummy, giving a squeal. I can't help but chuckle.

"Sadist!" she grumbles.

I watch as she slips from the mattress to the floor, standing at the foot of the bed, straightening the skirt into place. I reach over and fix the pigtails and the ribbons, since they've gone rather crooked. She goes to slap my hands away, but I stop her with a tender kiss, before continuing.

Her phone alerts me to an incoming video chat request from her youngest just as I'm considering a second kiss. This I've got to see, so I pass her the mobile, challenging her to answer it, dressed as she is.

To my surprise she does "Hey, what do you think, I'm embracing my inner teenager?" she asks brightly.

"You did a good job, Mum." comes her daughter's reply.

I roll my eyes, hold up five fingers denoting time, and leave the room. The conversation moves to her daughters cooking, they giggle and then Jess explains how to cook toasted grill cheese. Minutes later, she's makes her excuses and hangs up with her "love you, chat later" promise.

She's in the hallway, with time to spare.

"She knows about my little and not so little alters" she shrugs.

Taking her hand, guiding her out of the house, and over to the passenger side of the Tahoe outside. She gets in and gingerly places herself on the seat. Reaching over her, I secure the seat belt, before closing

the door and entering the vehicle from the other side.

Tank's driving with Terry riding next to him, we have the local club members riding escort on our way to the small private airfield.

"I have to ask, are you a pain bunny?" Tank cuts

his eyes towards Jess.

"No, the technical term is flopping, it's an automatic defense mechanism, I can't control it." It's my Princess explaining it, she looks for permission before continuing "I learned a long time ago, not to fight back, the flop mechanism relaxes me, flooding me with endorphins, unless you keep me mindful of my surroundings, I kind of disappear, that's why I have to keep count."

"I won't go into the gory details, but my brother destroyed her, mentally, physically and then one day she just quit responding, and he tore her body apart, she's got scars that she'll never heal from it." I explain further as Jess turns her head away to watch the scenery as we continue our journey.

"It was Terry that figured out how to keep her present, thankfully." I send Tel a nod of appreciation.

"I didn't know it had a technical label until just now, she just fades and goes limp." Terry adds.

"Princess?" I check on her making sure she's still present.

"Yeah? My therapist explained the term to me just recently, everyone's heard of fight or flight, but it turns out there are other choices, flop is one of them." Turning her attention back to the outside world, she continues "freeze and friend make up the rest, they are all immediate, automatic and instinctive responses to fear."

"I'm the friend!" Terry announces.

"Sometimes." Jess replies "I used to think I was freezing up, but my therapist explained that when you freeze, you go rigid and I do the opposite, I just go limp."

Tank turns into the parking area of the local private airstrip. The escort is checking the building out, we wait patiently for the all-clear, before heading into the tiny terminal area. Our pilot and co-pilot are already in the aircraft and finishing their checks ready to take us to Charlotte, North Carolina.

Jessica, still stiff and sore, walks in her heels between Terry and me. Climbing the stairs onto the plane I get a great view of the pattern Tank painted on her rear. He said a one month and I'll not allow her to heal them before that. She sits just as gingerly as before in the small private jet, securing the lap belt, before turning her attention to the outside world once more.

I give Tank my thanks as he helps close the door, sealing Terry, Jess and I inside. The pilot and co-pilot are members also, after checking on the door. They waste no time, getting us in the air. Jessica is still very quiet, and it unnerves me, I prefer her when she's outspoken and loud, I feel down our connection, it's peaceful between us.

"Princess?"

"I'm good, do I get to know where we're headed now?" she asks cautiously.

"Home."

"In this?" her heckles are up loud and proud now.

"No! We'll be catching a commercial flight out of Charlotte."

The engines purr loudly as we run the short runway, and then we climb. I have our passports in my backpack, assumed names with clean backgrounds for immigration. Jessica and I will fly first class transatlantic, Terry in the less spacious economy.

Jess

Going through passport control in Charlotte, I assume the identity I'm handed, Mrs. Emily Wilson, naturally Ronald is my husband. Terry is tailing us a couple of passengers back. We get through security without issue and head straight to the gate, we don't have more than a few minutes and they are calling for boarding.

Ron and I board in the first group, apparently Mrs. Wilson has priority as she's disabled. Although I can clearly register the disbelief on the agent's face as we pass through, Ron hands her my boarding card, as I stand silently next to him, our hands intertwined.

We're seated in the last row of first class, Ron has given me the window seat, knowing that I get travel sick if I can't see where we're going, even if it's only clouds, we're flying through.

Terry winks at me, as he boards with the other passengers heading to the back, where leg room means he'll spend the flight pinned up against the seat in front of him. I know it's nice to be boarded first, but it's never made much sense to have to sit there while people try not to bump into you as they pass by on their way to the back of plane, kids squawking and bags getting stuck. The line stops several times as passengers find their seats and stow their carry-on luggage.

Finally, everyone is loaded, and the male air hostess starts the emergency briefing, not that anyone is paying any attention. Still he's trying to add humor to his spiel to at least get a few laughs, as he explains the gas masks that will extend if needed. I turn my attention to the crew outside, they are still loading bags into cargo. I wonder for a moment how many souls we have on board, it's not a direction I should be focusing on.

With the aisle now free of passengers, the air hostess is asking first class if we want a warm towel. I shake my head no, but Ron takes one and asks for one for me as well. I ignore him, reaching up to adjust the in-flight air thingy my way and open it up fully.

Leaning in towards the window, I watch as we pull away from the gate and join the line for departure, I try to count the number of planes between us and the end of the runway, ignoring Ron as he double checks my seat belt is firmly in place.

Watching one plane after another, speeding down the runway, taking into the air, I try to remember the last time I made this flight. I had been alone, an emergency flight home to see my dad, just prior to his death. That had been thirteen years ago, I'd come home on a cheap flight funded by my mother-in-law and discounted as a bereavement flight by the airline.

Only a handful of people even knew I was home, unfortunately, I couldn't stay long enough to see my him buried, but I know where he is. Momentarily I wonder if I'll be able to visit his grave. The engines are revving now, it's our turn to speed up and climb into the clouds. I reach for Ron's hand, it's automatic as I hold my breathe. He gives my hand a gentle squeeze of understanding, we are pushed back in our seats as the plane begins to climb, the landing gear grinds as it rises below our feet, I breathe a sigh of relief.

Ron's still holding my hand, as we continue to climb, the pilot announces the flights cruising altitude, expected time of arrival and weather when we land in Gatwick, London. I slip my hand away from Ron's grasp and tilt my head to the window, closing my eyes, I hope he'll let me sleep.

The cabin lights are dimmed, when Ron nudges me for the hostess, she asks if I want anything to drink, I shake my head no, and try return to sleep.

"Princess, you should eat and drink something while we're in the air."

"Later" I mumble, sleep still so close.

I'm standing in the back of a lorry, the bread-man is talking to my dad, I begin the job of changing the wrapper from Tesco's to our store brand. If only our customers knew, the number of people who told my dad that his bread was better than Tesco's and it was day old Tesco bread the whole time. It's one of my morning duties in the shop before school, soon enough the Bread-man and Dad join me in the task. We take two racks, the bread-man hands them off the truck, in their new labels to my dad.

I follow them into the shop, a couple of kids are in the shop now, waiting to buy sweets. I go to the till and cash them out. The till is lethal, the cash drawer opens full throttle and if you're not careful it will take your fingers off when it closes.

I try to linger in the dream, but it moves on and I'm in the bus shelter outside, Terry is sitting next to me, we're laughing but I don't know why. Ron appears from nowhere, and then Terry flips backwards of the seat he'd been sitting on, I freeze, the anger rolling off Ron is dangerous. His fist connects with my face, he's got my throat in his hand as he does it, he's squeezing, he's so close to my face now, our noses about to touch. He pulls me from my seat and strikes my face a second time, releasing me to collapse on the dirty floor beneath me. His finger is pointed in my face, but I don't comprehend his words.

I'm awake, Ron's hand is on my thigh, the hot towel is on the tray in front of, I unfold it, it's still warm and I use it to wipe my face. I touch where Ron struck me in the dream, the memory of the attack fresh,

I feel the remnants of pain, deep in my muscle memory. Folding the towel neatly, placing it back on the tray, I adjust my position in the seat, the lap belt doesn't allow for much movement, Ron has is so secure.

I contemplate removing it, but I feel Ron run his hand along my thigh and decide not to. I close my eyes once more, praying that I sleep without dreaming for a while.

Ron

I watch as Jessica sleeps, she is sending me pictures of the shop her dad once owned, I only recall a handful of times that I ever crossed the threshold of the shop, but I'm seeing it through her eyes. I feel the happiness she is feeling as she helps her father with the morning duties.

The scene fades as I feel her soul try to cling to the memory, pain flows through our connection as the shop disappears. The next scene opens with laughter, I recognize the familiarity of the bus stop, and unfortunately the smell of stale urine, that's soaked into the brick work. Then I see me, I've knocked Terry for six and turned my attention to Jess, I feel my fingers wrap around her slender neck and squeeze, I feel the rage pouring out of me.

I pull away from our connection, I remember this day, and don't care to watch it from her point of view. Terry is new to our little club, he's more of a neighbor to Jess than I, he lives just a few streets over from her, while I live on the other side of town. I saw them laughing and thought she was two-timing me with this skinny runt of a boy. I gave him a shiner, and then I'd given her one to match, breaking my personal code of not hitting her where others can see. My hand closes around her throat, I hit her a second time and then pissed off at myself, I'd dropped her.

I recall screaming in her face that she belonged to me and that next time I'd kill her, before storming off, leaving the love birds to console each other.

Squeezing lightly on her thigh, I wake her from the memory, as she stirs, I gently rub her thigh, I watch as she wipes her face with the hot towel I got for her, even though she'd refused it. She's shifting next to me, trying to find a better position, maybe I should loosen the lap belt, but then she settles again, her eyes close once more, her breath steady.

She's exhausted, sleep comes fast. I see the air hostess coming back down the aisle, this time it's food she's offering, I select for both of us and ask for a Pepsi for Jessica as well. The hostess offers a blanket for Jess, which I accept gratefully. I know Jess won't wrap herself in it, the air is blasting down on as she's always hot, but maybe she'll make a pillow out of it, later in the flight.

I let her sleep for an hour, before waking her, she's a grumpy little witch when she wakes, but the food and drink help. Then she accepts the blanket, using it as a pillow and falls back to sleep, leaning as before away from me.

This time I settled down to try to get some rest myself. The connection between is open, images of things that make no sense float by. A kid is climbing into the back of a boat, covering himself with a blue tarp, he has a black backpack with him. A woman driving a red ford fiesta, I hear Jess screaming for her to turn left, she doesn't and then that's gone as well. I'm walking now, across marshy turf, I see bodies below the earth, girls, women and one pregnant female.

Jess stirs, shifts again, then her head is on my shoulder, she's sleeping deeply for now. For a long time, the movie clips cease as we both slept peacefully.

"This is your captain speaking, we will be landing soon, please place your trays in the up-right position as flight crew prepare for landing."

The announcement wakes us both, I had hoped I could have spent the flight time getting reacquainted with Jess in a non-threatening manner, but she is exhausted. I never understood until now, just what it was like to be her, see the things she sees. Angel of death she calls herself, but it's so much more, she sees the end of things. However, having hidden from her gift, the images are fragmented, important details needed to call the authorities are often missing.

When she'd been younger the Watchers and vampires had worked with her, hoping to teach her how to use her gift with more skill, but Christopher would terrorize her for any information she may have shared after every teaching session. Eventually, Jessica closed down; refusing to listen to her tutors, I was forced to punish her for not cooperating. It's no wonder she fell so completely apart, with all that we did to her.

Unlike take-off, Jessica doesn't reach for my hand during landing, she's repeatedly swallowing trying to pop her ears as we make our slow descent, the city comes into view below as she watches us getting closer to the ground below. The landing gear whirls once again as it descends, then we hit the runway below, the brakes and flaps slow us rapidly. Looking down, she's fisting her hands together, then rubbing her wrists absently as we begin to taxi to the terminal.

Reaching over, I unclip the lap belt, as she continues to watch as we approach the terminal. Feeling down our connection, I feel her resignation as we crawl towards the building.

Rubbing her face with one hand she looks over at me "I'm fine."

I nod in reply.

Jess

Getting through security, collecting the rental afterwards and getting onto the open road goes smoothly, it feels strange to be home after all this time, we're headed north back towards the place I grew up. I called shotgun at the rental counter, so Terry is stuck sitting in the rear passenger section by himself, as Ron drives us out of the rental parking area.

Claustrophobia grips me as we enter traffic, it happened the last time I was home also, everything here is clustered together closely, I've grown used to the wide-open space of my American home. Ron's driving a manual, but between shifting gears, his hand rest on my thigh, the connection helps me stay grounded.

Sitting in companionable silence, I focus on the road ahead, thankful Ron is taking it easy at least for now, and driving without aggression with the flow of traffic, out and away from the airport traffic. It's unnerving having traffic on the wrong side of the vehicle, last time I'd been home, I'd done the driving.

Back then, I'd been going south, as my parents had moved to the south coast to enjoy their retirement. Pulling onto the M23, we are joined by a group of bikers, continuing up towards the Dartford tunnel/bridge area, I notice we've picked up a different group of bikers. Paying attention to the patches the riders wear, as we go further north, I notice two more changes to the patches our faceless escorts wear. Finally, we're being escorted by patches I recognize, the skull and snakes of the one percenters I grew up around bring uncomfortable memories.

These are Ron's family, not mine, glancing at the Eeyore tattoo, his feet just peeking out from under the sleeve of my shirt, I grin. I wonder how much longer it'll be till Ron discovers my disregard for club rules, although it's not a club tat, so technically doesn't break any club rules. It's a grey line for sure, depending on Ron's mood when he sees it.

"Um? Can we make a pit stop?" Not long after we make the change from M11 to the A11, I know we're closing in our destination, but my bladder is complaining painfully.

"We're about thirty minutes out."

"I'm not going to make it." I whine, my little close to the surface.

"Sorry Baby, you'll have to hold it."

"Please!"

"Tel, let them know we're doubling back to the shell station." Ron gives me a look, "Little one?"

"Yes, Daddy?" my voice has gone up a pitch, matching my little's energy, she's in full control, I'm being forced to take the back seat in this confused body of ours.

"Hold it a little longer, baby." Both of Daddy's hand are on the steering wheel as he makes the U-turn.

"Can you hold it for Daddy, baby?"

"I'll try." I promise.

Every bump has me squirming, I squeeze my legs tightly together, as we race back the way we came, the scary bikers are chasing us, Daddy is cross with me. His energy is scary! I try to make myself tiny as we travel, his grip on the steering wheel it tight. I want to climb in the back seat with Terry, but that'll only make Daddy madder, he hates when I get comfort from Terry instead of my Daddy. I see the gas station come into view, it's not far now, looking over at Daddy, his expression is stern and he's making me nervous, but I can't help it, I need to pee. Jessie should have told him earlier, maybe I should let her talk to Daddy. But she's gone for now, it's just me here.

I curl my legs in underneath me, as Daddy parks

and comes over to my side of the car. He looks really annoyed.

"Little one, what's wrong?" I try to disappear into the seat, as he reaches over me to release the seat belt "baby girl?"

"I'm sorry Daddy!" I cry.

"Did you have an accident baby?" his voice doesn't match his energy, it's tender and concerned.

"No, Daddy."

"Then what you sorry for?

"Making you mad."

"I'm not mad at you, little one, come on." He scoops me into his arms, heading inside the shell station "You want Daddy to come in with you and help?" he whispers into my ear as he carries to the back of convenience area, towards the toilet.

"No Daddy, I'm a big girl."

"Hmm?" he sets me down gently, holds the door open for me "remember to wash your hands, baby girl."

I nod as I scurry to the toilet, I hear the door close behind me, after taking care of my needs, I head straight for the door, Daddy is still standing on the other side of it.

"Hands?"

"Oops!" I run over to the sink and wash them with soap. Before heading back out, both my hands are still wet as the paper dispenser is empty. I wipe them on my skirt, before taking Daddy's hand.

"Better?"

I nod, and follow him over to the counter, he's buying cigarettes and lets me choose a pack of gummy bears. But I'm not allowed them until we get home, I pout but he looks cross again, as we head back to the car.

"Get in little one."

I climb in the front seat and then between the front seats to get in the back with Terry, he's my friend, I'm almost through, when Daddy's hand connects with my rear, it makes me jump and I lose my footing, slipping headfirst into Terry's lap.

Terry helps me onto the back seat, looking up, I see a large smile covers Daddy's face "fine." He says, as Terry slides me from the center seat to the passenger seat. He slips the seat belt in place and takes the center seat himself. Placing his arm over my shoulders, I lean down and lay in his lap, as Daddy gets back in the driver's seat. He gives me a quick look, shakes his head and reverses out of the shell station.

I close my eyes and enjoy the gentle stroking of Terry's hand down my thigh. Moments later I'm asleep. I dream I'm sleeping with Lucky my dog wrapped over me, he's a shepherd mix of some kind, he used to be a latch key dog, basically a stray dog during working hours, but a family dog in the evenings, with his previous family. But he's my dog now, and he protects me, he never leaves my side and listens to my commands without exception. Mum says she can't hold him on the leash he's too powerful for her and Dad uses a choke chain on him, says I'm not allowed to take him out of the house on walks as he's always starts a fight with other dogs when Dad walks him. But I take him with me whenever I can, I do take the leash, but it's never latched to his collar, I don't need it and it's our secret.

Ron

Concentrating on the road ahead, I glance several times into the backseat, Jess is comfortable and seems peaceful in Terry's lap. Jealousy of their relationship courses through my veins, their relationship has always been so carefree and easy. It's painful to watch, I know that Jess has no sexual attraction for him, but I'm not so sure Terry feels the same way.

I think back to what she was saying earlier about the flight or fight thing, she said that Terry was a friend but only sometimes, I wonder if that's because she knows he's loyal to me first. I recall how she acted when she'd run from the back of my bike earlier and onto him, her grip so tight. Envious fire builds in my heart. I turn my attention to the road to calm down.

I pull onto the B road and then down the long tree lined lane that leads to the manor house, glancing in the backseat, as I pull to a stop in front of the house, Jess is fast asleep. I don't want to disturb her,

"You good here mate?" I ask.

"Sure." Terry nods with understanding.

Our escort all pull into the connected garage round the back, which is where I head, leaving Jess where she is for a while with Terry.

Entering the large garage through the front door, the guy's meander over a few at a time as they stow their bikes and gear.

"James, Henry?" I swing my head towards the manor.

They follow me as I make my way over to the back office. I'm still uncomfortable thinking of it as my office. I take a seat on the dark leather high backed lounger, preferring it to my brother's chair behind the heavy oak desk. James and Henry, both grab me individually with a quick arm press hug and then sit opposite sharing the matching two-seater opposite.

I've been keeping them up to date on Jessica's progress, "She's a fucking mess!" I announce exasperated

to my oldest buddies "I've left her sleeping in Tel's lap." Frustrated I get up and pace, I feel like a caged animal.

"At least she's home now." James comments.

"Yeah! Not sure where she's at with it though, right before we left the safe house, she stole Tank's ride, took off blinded by fear, and it wasn't for me."

"Yeah, Terry filled us in on that!"

"I didn't even know she could ride!" I prop myself against the edge of Chris's desk, my fingers gripping the edge like I'm holding it up "Has Stan found anything on this Rubec?"

"He found one of her properties close by, but couldn't confirm if she is in residents, apparently, she is known as the serpent queen among the vamps. House of Gorgon and she's as twisted as they come, Guv!"

"Yeah, like fucking Medusa!" Henry adds.

Steven walks in with a nod just then "Tel's got a bit of problem outside mate" he says casually "want me to take over?"

"Nah mate!" I sigh "I've got it." pushing myself to my feet, I head towards the front door. A number of the guys are observing and egging the commotion on.

I can't believe my eyes when I see what has them all riled up, Jess is sitting across Terry's chest, laying punches into his bloodied face. Terry's trying his best to fend her off, but she's a wildcat for every punch she lands, several more hit the gravel next to him. I let her have a few more good strikes since it warms my insides to see him take the beating from my Princess.

Walking over she doesn't even register me, I wrap my arms around her waist and pull her off him, her arms still swinging wildly. "That's enough!" the crowd is still cheering "Jessica, enough!"

"Fuck off! Let me go!"

I gather one of her arms into my hold, reaching for the second, I feel teeth bite into the back of my hand.

"Ow! I said that's enough!" I growl. Dropping to my knees, I pin her beneath me.

"Terry?" Finally, I have both her arms pinned under me and she's stopped fighting me "Explain?"

"Hell, if I know" Terry states at the same time as Jess says, "he was fucking groping me!"

"I never!"

"The hell you weren't!" Jess is twisting again beneath me "Get fuck off me, Wanker!"

"Want help Guv!" Steven offers.

"Screw You!" Jess replies

"Terry, go get sorted, Steve mate! Piss off!" I look over at the crowd, they waste no time clearly off, "Now Witch? Settle the fuck down!" I complete the sentence as forcefully as I could muster into her angry face.

I don't need to look through our connection to see her flip through identities, her features and mood switching every few seconds or so.

"Princess? Baby?" I inquire as she seems to settle beneath me, then I'm riding a raging bull once more, I pin her with my full length and weight, until she stops again.

"Daddy, you're squishing me." A little voice cries as she settles once more.

"Baby Girl?"

"Yes, Daddy."

I start to lift my weight "Sucker!" a much deep voice calls, as her form pushes up against me, and rolls out from under me. I recover quickly, grabbing her ankle preventing her from getting up. I roll over her and now I'm sitting on her back, her head behind me, her arms under her chest, I hear her "oomph!" as she expels the air trapped in her lungs as I sit back heavily.

"Guardian?"

"Not buying it!" her skirt has twisted to her middle and her arse is exposed, the strips Tank applied earlier still visible, I smack her sharply over them.

"You're not my type!" comes the deep voice again, then I feel her struggle for freedom. I feel for our connection, but it's gone dark, wherever the Witch is she's no longer home, neither is my Princess. It's blank, void of anything, I try to pull her power forward, but it's empty.

"No ones home motherfucker!" She's pushing up against me.

Sitting back on my hunches, I unclasp my belt, wrap the buckle into my palm and then start criss-crossing her rear intent on beating whoever lies below me into submission. "Count!"

I'm not keeping track of my strikes, and this alter isn't either, I work my strikes further down, catching the tender skin of her upper thighs and seat. Still, I'm met with silence, this just fuels my determination.

She's bucking under me once more, I scoot higher up her length, sitting across her shoulders, my butt holding her face in the gravel. She's kicking her legs wildly, but I'm confident she's not going anywhere as I strike her lower back, until she stills again. I pause then, gathering my strength and conviction for another volley, I inch back down her length a little as I decide on a new, more tender target. Unwrapping a few inches of the belt, I judge the distance to my target and having lined it up as best as I'm able in this position, with her still silent and still below me, I aim and fire. My belt lands right between the cheeks, the tip dipping low between her juicy bulbs.

Instantly she's gone limp below me, I rise just enough to prevent me from completely cutting off her airway and take aim for a second time. Aim as true as the first, I apply three more in the exact same place. I feel energy buzz through our connection, its jolt electrifying my internal core.

"Count!"

I strike again, and finally Jessica's voice replies

"One Guardian."

Relief washing through me, as I apply four more, each one is accompanied by her count, I lift my weight off her and she doesn't move. "Roll over, Jess" I instruct. Once she's on her back, I sit on her tummy

lightly, and strike her lightly with the tip of the belt, right on her clitoris. Her sharp intake of air confirming how close she was to coming, her voice shaky, she continues her count.

Because I'm a fucking bastard, I get off her without finishing the job, holding out a hand, I help Jess to her feet. Her shoes discarded at some point during all this commotion, I pick them up and escort her with a hand around her waist into the house, guiding her upstairs and into my bedroom.

Testing our connection, everything seems to be back in place, as Jessica seems to be in control once more, gesturing towards a chair. "Wait there." I instruct as I go into the toilet outside the room and gather a wet cloth.

She's still standing when I return to the room, not that I blame her, I can smell her arousal and see the welts a mix of old and new.

"I'm married, you know?"

"I'm aware." Wiping the remaining gravel and dirt from the side of her face gently.

"I love him."

Tears threaten to fall, as I brush whispers of loose hair back to their respective sides.

"He needs me."

"I hear you, Princess." straightening her pigtails and ribbons."You're mine, you've always been mine!" pulling the skirt down the length of her legs, I guide it free."Place, baby girl."

Her features tighten, looking me in the eyes, she holds the connection, and she drops to her knees in front of me. Her hands reach up automatically, her fingers release my cock from its confines. Eyes on me, she opens her lips and guiding with her hands she takes me, twisting her tongue around the tip, she settles into old habits. Her fingers guide, encourage and combine with her tongue to engulf me in sensation. As pressure builds, I take control of her head, increasing my depth, entering her throat and backing out, controlling her breathing, as my tension builds. I know she's doing everything to bring me to quick completion, but I slow her progression, enjoying the sensation for as long as I can bare.

My rhythm building, staying further down her between her tonsils as I near the end, choking her with my member. Jess shivers as I explode coating her throat with my milk. I pull back, resting my cock on her tongue, her eyes still on me, I nod, and she begins to clean me completing the ritual.

"You belong to me."

Jess

He's taken my freedom with his words, my mind is processing, he knows I'm married but he doesn't care, I'm his property, nothing has changed. I'm owned and now I'm trapped in a country I never thought I'd ever go back too.

My family, children, grandchildren and most painful of all, my husband out of my reach. I'm back in England under a fake name, with a fake husband. No money, no real identity, nothing to prove who I really am. Even if I could escape him, we are connected now, permanently, I'm so fucked!

I remain in the position he left me in, his cum still coats my mouth, a nasty reminder of his ownership, the strips of his belt still burning my skin. And Goddess; help me, I'm totally horny and ready for him to fulfill my desperate need.

He's my special version of heroin, I hate him, but I know I'd give him everything, I've always known I'd give myself to him. I can't help it, it's been trained into me, I flop under his hands and will do anything to please and befriend that evil bastard.

Footsteps outside the room bring me back to the reality of the room, a single knock and then the door opens.

"You broke Terry's nose." Steven mentions as he sets down a tray on the table next to the window, crossing back towards the door, he looks down at me "better get cleaned up and eat."

Steven's the club's enforcer, Ron's best friend and a complete arsehole. I hate it when he's my minder, he enjoys intimidating me, twisting my response to his actions so I'm the guilty one. I don't trust anything he says or does, he thrives on my punishment and the control that threat affords him.

I wait for him to leave before moving, the discarded skirt, not looking so cute or welcoming anymore, I wished I'd not chosen these clothes. I reach up and begin to release the pigtails, placing the ribbons on the dresser next to me, I run my fingers through my hair, without the aid of a mirror it's the best I can to untangle my curls. Seeing no other option, I pull on the skirt, straightening my underwear beneath it.

Walking over to the table, I look out the window and see nothing but fields, I don't see anything recognizable, my fingers wrap around one half of the sandwich left for me by Mr. Nasty, I absently wonder if these windows open. At least the ham and pickle sandwich help to void the taste that remains in my mouth.

I take a look at the medication that's sitting in a small dish on tray, I've not been on my regular medication since I left work, I've fixed my outward bodily issues, but I should talk to Ron about my regular medication routine.

I'm eating the second half of the sandwich when I feel Ronald enter the room, I ignore him for now, still finishing the sandwich.

"Princess?"

"Guardian?"

"You take the pill?"

"Not yet, what are they?"

"Paracetamol, pain killers"

I look down at them again, trying to remember what their American equivalent is, but it's been so long I don't recall. "What's the active ingredient?"

"Huh?"

"What chemical is it? I can't take certain things 'cos I'm not well."

"That reminds me, the Doc will be by in the morning, he's got your medical records, he said those are safe for you, so take them."

"I'm good."

"Just for once, can you do as you're told without a fight."

"Fine!" I gather the pills and the orange juice on

the tray, face him and make a show of taking the pills, I stick out my tongue after I swallow them to proof, they are gone "There!"

He shakes his head in mild amusement. "Put your shoes on, we're going to get you some new clobber."

Looking at the heels, they truly are the last thing I want to put back on, but with no other options, I do as he asks, hoping that my new outfits include some trainers.

With his hand draped over my shoulder, we exit into the hallway and down the stairs, Terry is at the bottom, his nose is taped, and his eyes are unhealthy colors. He reaches for my hand as we get close

"Did I?" he nods "Sorry." He nods again, giving my hand a quick squeeze before letting go. James is holding the car door open when we go outside, with Steven already in the driver's seat, I climb in the back seat without complaint. Ron secures the belt around me, and we're headed along the lane.

We turn onto a B road and then onto the A11, the sign reads as we make the turn. We're headed into my hometown, seeing a mix of familiar and new stores as we roll down the High Street.

Steven pulls over in front of what was the co-op, now it's something called 'New Look', Ron and I get out, once the door closes, Steven pulls away and back into traffic. Ron holds the door like a gentleman for me, as I pass his arm wraps around my middle, we make our way over the ladies' section, he starts to thumb through the racks, holding some items up against me to test the look and fit.

A full length bright green dress catches my eye, but he shakes his head when I point in its direction. A shop assistant joins us, she introduces herself as Teresa, I ask her where the shoe section is located, and she walks us over.

Ron selects another pair of heels; these ones are open toed.

"I'd prefer trainers?"

An evil grin washes over his face "My money, Princess."

"Don't be mean." I plead.

He laughs, and gives permission for me to find trainers, I'm reading the American size on the box, hoping that they fit. Ron leads me over to the changing rooms, his arms loaded with an assortment of items.

Teresa is back and helps me into a fitting room, thankfully she tells him, men aren't allowed in the female rooms. Naturally he demands to see each outfit, giving each a thumbs up or down based on his opinion of how I look in them. I tell him when I'm in the last outfit and he hands me the green dress, I saw earlier to put on, but he also hands the heels he'd selected with it.

I pull a face, which earns me a tap to my tender bottom, as I reenter the changing area, to try on the dress and the shoes. Twirling on the shop floor, Ron gives the outfit, two thumbs up. Knowing my English size now, makes picking out undies easier. Teresa seeing a large commission check, helps by measuring my new perking boobs.

Ron hands over his credit card, Teresa is beaming as she packs my new wardrobe into large bags. "Where now baby?" He surprises me.

"Boots!"

"Boots?"

"Yeah, a girl needs things."

Realization dawns, as he gathers the bags into one hand and me into his other. We walk a way up the High Street, it feels so natural to be back in his arms, under his protection. Reaching Boots, he briefly lets go and holds the door once again, allowing me to enter. Then his arm is lazily around my shoulders, he allows me to guide him towards the feminine section, I select a couple of different products, then we walk the rest of the store, as I choose a hairbrush, and other sanitary products.

It's not until we are unloading my second haul of the day at the register, that I notice he's added a long handled back scrubber made of sturdy wood and a flat backed much smaller wooden hairbrush. Leaving the chemist, I'm once again tucked in close to his side, both his hands now weighted down with my shopping.

We're headed towards the car park, Steven has the engine running, but James comes over and takes the bags, loading them into the boot, as Ron guides me into the backseat once more. I'm not familiar with the side street we travel down, we've gone a different way, and now we're deep in a neighborhood on Ron's side of town. Most of these houses used to be council owned, but I know some were sold off to tenants during Thatcher's rein.

We pull to the curb, the garden to the bungalow is well kept, and the wall that separates it from the pavement is painted purple. Ron gets out first, and then lends a hand for me to exit his side of the car. He takes my hand and leads me up the cobble stone path to the extension glass sliding door.

"Ronald." An elderly lady, dressed in a pretty pink dress, which has puffy sleeves embraces him at the door, just as we reach it.

"Florence, this is my little Princess, as I explained on the phone, she's in need of some outfits."

I look between the two, confused for a moment as she ushers us into the house, we follow her into a bedroom, she has several racks of adult baby and little girl and boy clothing. I feel my cheeks heat as I take in the choices.

"So how old is your little Princess?"

"Her Brat is preteen." Ron points to my current outfit, as I fight the need to stick my tongue out at him

"Her little is around five or six."

"So, she's potty trained?"

"We might need some night time pull ups, she's prone to night time accidents." He comments, as my cheeks go an even brighter shade of red, which I feel go down my neck.

"No need for embarrassment, baby girl, let mummy help find you some nice party dresses." She walks me over to a circular rail that is full of fully skirted puffy sleeved dresses.

"Maybe Daddy, would like to take a look at some toys while we girls find you items that make her feel like a real Princess?"

Ron nods and she tells him where to look in her living room. Meanwhile she lets me look through the cute dresses. I'm still so embarrassed, I'm not really looking, moving along I see a coloring book and crayons sitting on the table in the corner.

"Would it be easier if you just let me pick, baby girl?" I nod making a beeline for the table. "You go ahead sweetie, make yourself comfortable, coloring, I'm good at guessing sizes."

I'm halfway coloring an Easter bunny holding a basket of eggs, when Daddy comes to collect me, he sits down next to me while I finish. "Ready?"

"Yup!"

"Bring those with you."

We leave Ms. Florence house with several boxes, I haven't tried anything on, so I hope that things fit, she's a sweet lady, and gives me a motherly hug before waving us goodbye from her doorway. Sitting in the back seat, I feel Jessica take control.

"Ron?"

"Yes, Princess."

"How long do you plan to keep me here?"

"You have a job to do."

"Yes." I reply, scared that he's planning on forever.

Elizabeth

I 've lost count of how many days and nights I've been trapped here. The small serving hatch opens twice a day, then I'm allowed two trips to the toilet. Rubec hasn't visited for a long time, I'm kept naked in this silver box, with a concrete floor. I can't prop myself against the walls, and I can't stretch put fully either, as it's only ten steps to any wall.

My wolf has settled for now, she wore herself out trying to escape this cell, her claw marks by the hatch the only proof she even tried.

The last serving of rations, sits on the tray, I'm on hunger strike in protest. I know Rubec won't let me starve to death. I am her favorite pet, well at least I used to be. That was before I escaped her the first time, I'd run feral from my pack then as well.

Thinking about the pack, stirs my wolf again. She blames me for our current situation, she wants to be with her mate. I'm not going back I tell her again. She's close to the surface, but I'm not letting her out to slam us into the cell walls endlessly. It serves neither of us to be battered and broken at our own hands, I remind her.

'But we can starve!' she shoots back.

I remind her; Rubec, loves us and it won't be much longer, but honestly, I'm not so sure, but I hide that thought from my wolf.

A hand reaches through the hatch and removes the tray, it's quickly replaced with a new one. Wolf is hungry, the smell of bacon wafts in our direction.

I turn my back to the tray, hug myself into a ball of determination, the scent will fade into the background soon enough. My stomach twists and grumbles painfully in complaint of my decision.

The little red light on the camera above us, steadily blinks, I know someone is watching, as I stare back at them. I sit so long in one place; my body no longer feels the cold or the roughness of the floor. I stare at the stupid red light, my heartbeat in time with its blinking.

Ron

Jess goes silent after I don't answer her question fully, I know she's thinking of her old life, I feel the emotion traveling between our connection. I want to pull her into my arms and comfort her but it seems a little sadistic when I'm the one causing the pain. Seeing her sitting in Florence's house coloring she was so darn adorable; I wish I could be the Daddy she really needs. Still, I can't wait to see the look on her little's face when she sees her new dresses.

Maybe I can take her to a tea party, so she can make some local friends with similar tastes, I muse.

"Tea Party?"

"Um? Yes, would you like that?" I didn't think I'd said that out loud, was this something we could do now.

We're parked outside the manor once more, the guys have left us, James is unloading the boot, Jess releases her seat belt. She's leaning away from me, "We need to find Elizabeth first, then I'll take you to a party, I promise."

"She's on hunger strike!"

"Who is?"

"Lizzy!"

"It's not far."

It's my little Princess and not the Witch relaying the information, she goes quite, like she's straining to hear someone in the distance.

"It's cold, hard silver, her wolf is very unhappy."

"Can I talk to the Witch, Baby?"

She's shaking her head before I even finish my question "I want to play dress up first!"

With that she's opens her door and sprints towards the house, shaking my own head, a broad smile on my face, I give chase, quickly catching up with her, I pick her up and toss her over my shoulder as she squeals in my ear.

I take the stairs, two steps at time, kicking the bedroom door open we startle James who has just finished delivering the boxes from Ms. Florence's. I sit on the side of the bed, setting her gently in space in front of me. Reaching behind me, I grab the first box in reach, it has a pretty blue ribbon tied around it.

Jess pulls the longer end free, and the bow unties. I help her remove it completely, then I tease her, opening the lid to the box and peaking in so she can't see what's inside. She's so cute trying to pry my hands out of the way, that I allow it and she tosses the lid behind her. I pop the end of her nose in warning, her eyes go wide as her hands separates the blue tissue to the side.

The party dress inside is lemon colored with blue and white swirled lollipops decorating it. Her entire face lights up, I take it and shake the layers of ruffles that make up the skirt part. It has a two-inch satin pale blue ribbon sewn around the middle, short puff sleeves, and scooped neckline finish the dress perfectly.

"Go put it on baby and put these on under it." I hand her a bag containing frilly knickers, and ankle socks to match.

She kicks off the red soled heels, before leaving the bedroom, I can't help the shake of my head, as she skips into the bathroom across the way. Moments later she's twirling away in front of me. I notice she's fidgeting with her wedding ring, slipping it halfway off then twisting and pushing it on again.

"Can I go play?"

"Don't get it dirty and no going outside." I caution before allowing her to show off her new dress. "No running!" I call after her, as she takes off at top speed, no doubt looking for Terry.

I hear her squeal as she finds him, somewhere downstairs, as I turn my attention to putting all her clothes away in the space, I've already prepped for her. I leave the pull ups on top of my dresser and stash the new bedroom toys in my toy drawer.

The guy's downstairs are amused by her display, the older members having had experience with her, play along and even start a game of It. Most of the newer members are perplexed by her excitement, and who could blame them she's manic, one moment she's punching the crap out of a member, the next she's a little girl showing off her new party dress.

Steve's watching from a distance, we both know she'll not stay little around him, seeing me he heads towards the garage. Terry is currently 'It' and she's really making it hard for him to catch her, so he tags me in. Now I'm 'It', only Jess thinks it's still Terry, I creep up behind her and tag her "You're It!"

"No fair!" she complains, but then takes off after one of our young apprentices as he heads for the stairs

"You're It!" she squeals.

The game comes to an end when she dramatically falls on the floor backwards and announces she doesn't want to play anymore. Terry goes over to help her up "You're It!" she squeals.

"Now Jessie, we've talked about cheating before!" she pouts but apologizes sweetly. I call the official end of the game.

Jess

Daddy's a real spoilsport, after he calls the end to our game, he sends me to go find big girl clothes. I slam the door to the bedroom behind, before I start opening drawers, the top drawer is full of Daddy's things, the one below is also his things.

I move to the next dresser, here I find the things we bought in the first shop, I get out a matching set of black lace underwear and toss them on the bed. Next drawer I find a pair of jeans, and below that a t-shirt.

On top of Daddy's dresser is a pair of scissors, I check the door is closed, and then cut the legs off the jeans, making myself a pair of daisy dukes, I fray the edge a little with my fingers pulling at threads.

Satisfied with the way they look; I take the party dress off and lay it gently on the bed. Touching it, it's so pretty, I wish I could wear it all day every day. Removing the frilly knickers, I toss them into the corner, along with the discarded jeans legs, I leave my socks on, and add the bralette and lacy underwear I picked out. Pulling the daisy dukes on, I adjust them so I'm not getting a wedgy, then I gather the t-shirt material in the front, tucking it up and under between my tits, so that my tummy is exposed.

Finding my new hairbrush, I gather my hair into a ponytail, securing it with the butterfly clip I got at the chemist. I wish there was a mirror in the room, but I figure the outfit works. Leaving the room, the dresser drawers still open, I make my way down the stairs and into the kitchen, where I can hear Ron's voice.

A chorus of wolf whistles follow me into the kitchen, Ron beckons me over, so I give him a twirl.

"Where'd you get those?"

"I made them, you like?" I tease.

"Sit down!"

He's trying to sound mad, but he is finding it hard not to laugh, the side of his mouth curling up, he shakes his head at me.

"You'll be the death of me." He complains as I choose to sit on his lap.

"Maybe?"

"You're on your own their mate!" Steven says as he passes Ron a plate of chips.

"Sit still" Ron fusses as I wiggle purposefully in his lap.

I steal one of his chips, dip in his ketchup and look

up at him, as I make show of swallowing, like it's a little snake.

"Seriously?"

"What? I'm hungry too!"

"I'll give you something else to eat, if you don't settle down and behave." He warns.

I don't think I want the thing he's suggesting, I try to move to safety. But he holds me in place, grinning down at me.

"Settle, have a chip." He dips the one he's holding in ketchup and offers it too me.

I eat out of his fingers gently; he feeds us both then as I settle. The hand that previously held me in place drops between my thighs, he presses lightly along the seam of my crotch, lazily.

The guys pay less notice too us, as they get involved in their own conversations. Daddy is feeding me a hot dog now. His hand has left my crotch and is lifting my right sleeve.

"So, what's Eeyore doing on your arm, Baby?" he asks softly, as I chew on the section of hot dog and bun he just fed me.

"He's holding three balloons, one for each of my grand babies." I tell him honestly "Eeyore represents me." I clarify.

"Eeyore's the depressed one, right?"

"Yeah." I confirm leaning forward in hopes for another bite.

"Daisy dukes, Tats, and I'm betting when we go upstairs, you've left a mess."

"Maybe?" I confess.

He offers me another bite of the hot dog, his hand traveling back to my crotch.

"After we finish here, you're going to go tidy the room, put away your party dress in the closet and be in corner, nose to wall when I join you."

I nod, as I continue to chew on the last section of my hot dog.

"Young lady?"

"Yes, Daddy." I agree, hurrying to finish the mouthful I have left.

I watch quietly as he finishes his own hot dog. His thumb still teases me though the daisy dukes.

"Go on, be a good girl, Jessie." He advises me as he helps me off his lap.

Turning I plant a kiss on his cheek, before heading back to the bedroom. It really doesn't take much time to close the drawers, hang the party dress, and put the cut off sections of the jeans in the bin. I find the laundry basket in the bathroom, I toss the frilly knickers in it, taking the opportunity to take care of my own needs as I do. Walking back into the room, everything is in order, even the scissors are back where I found them earlier.

Since he didn't tell me exactly where to stand, I choose the corner closest to the window, that way I can see outside while I wait. There's a lot of activity in the back yard now, biker bunnies are dancing with a few of the members, the music classic soft rock, fills the air.

I watch as a few of the member's strip bare, and then transform into wolves, it's not the first time I've witnessed shifters change, but I am surprised that the club now allows non-human members.

"I could have sworn I said corner and not window?"

I jump at his voice, placing my nose against the wall in front of me.

"Nice try" his hands take a firm but not painful grip of my shoulders "now let's, see? Which corner?"

Ronald makes a show, of putting me in each corner, checking whether it works for him, before he finally settles on the most boring corner in the room. Void of windows, and far enough away from the door, I have to rely on my senses to know where he is in the room.

I follow the sounds he's making as I stand like a statue, he's opening and closing drawers. I hear the sound of a package or two being cut by scissors. I burn to see to what he's doing, but my butt still carries

the scars of the past two days, I really don't want to receive any more punishments tonight.

"I promise you pleasure, little girl, but you owe me vengeance."

I know not to speak when I'm in the corner, unless given instructions otherwise, but this new skill we seem to have is something I'm still learning about. Christopher and I never spoke to each other this way.

Concentrating on our connection I test "Can you hear my thoughts?" Either he's ignoring me, or he didn't hear me, I try again, same question. Again, no response, huh?

"Sorry Princess? Did you say something?"

"You can hear me?"

"Sometimes, come here."

Turning slowly, I'm intoxicated by the familiarity of the scene before me, he's sitting in the high back smoking chair, black belted jeans his only clothing. My body moves with its own absolution, my brain screaming betrayal for my husband. Ronald's fingers encourage my approach, the space between while short, seems to take forever to cross. My little has gone, and I'm fighting with my inner brat for dominance, I stop just out of his reach.

"I hate you." I whisper.

"I know you do," He grins "but little girls who play with fire, get burnt. Now take that shirt off."

His eyes demand my commitment to his authority, as I remove the t-shirt, I'd previously styled to tease, his non-verbal signal to remove the bralette no surprise.

"Bend over the bottom of the bed."

My husband's image has me pausing, guilt washing through me, but I'm not home anymore, I'm on Ron's time now, my thighs and lower bottom stinging a new with the arousal coursing through my lower section, my feet propelling me into his desired position. Heat in my cheeks burns as I relax myself in a comfortable position.

Ron

Watching Jessica struggle with her submission as she complies with my requests reminds me how good we were once. She's a natural submissive, with two adorable entities for me to play with, but it's the real Jessica that is exposed right now, I see it in her expression, the turmoil, raging at the surface. I let her relax in her new position and watch her cheeks glow, knowing that the fire below burns for me.

I had planned on binding her in place, but forcing her submission without restraints is so much more for both of us. She's still fighting me for power and control in our daily interactions, keeping my dominant position will be a healthy lesson for both Jessica and the witch inside.

Taking my time, I step behind her, my fingers brushing the fading patterns of her earlier punishments, I watch her ball her fists in silent argument with herself. Removing my touch, I know increasing her arousal, I collect the braided flogger I'd purchased from Florence. Testing it across my own thigh, I test the weight of the blow and judge the sting like the skilled Dom I am.

Returning to Jess, I trail the tips of the leather along her spine, allowing her to prepare and anticipate the tool in her mind. I desire her to focus on the now, she can feel guilt afterwards but for now she is totally mine.

With feather light strikes; I coat her dixie short, covered rear, Jess relaxing signaling her automatic reaction "Remind me of your infractions?"

"Um, Teasing?"

"And?"

"Leaving a messy room."

"And?"

"Huh?"

I trail the tails of my weapon along the arm with the offending artwork as a reminder.

"Oh! Yeah, the ink"

"Yeah, the ink, it is cute, but a rule is still a rule, no matter how much freedom I may afford you!"

"Sir?"

"We'll call the tat ten, how much for the teasing Jess?"

"Don't be mean, you always enjoyed my littles in the past."

"True, but penance has to paid, so?"

"Ten Sir."

I flick a weighted strike across her tender thighs "Count, a rule is a rule."

"One, a rule is a rule, Sir." Her voice soft, as she repeats her count.

I take my time, aiming along the line between butt and thigh for the next four, each time is followed by her count "Now, teasing Daddy comes with a price, Princess."

Reaching underneath her, I release the button and zipper on the remains of the jeans, pulling them and the lacy knickers together, I free her of the materials. Stepping over to the toys I pulled out earlier and grabbing the lube. I show Jess the medium sized butt plug I intend to insert; it has a pretty purple heart jewel inlaid at the base. I place it in her hand so she can feel the weight of it.

Applying a good amount of lube, I work my thumb into her anus, no instruction is needed, we've played here before. I waste no time, replacing my thumb with the tip of the toy, I move it gently into place. I dip my fingers lower and find she's already sopping wet.

"You don't cum, my little Tease." I whisper the order as I dip three fingers and curl them, applying pressure with my palm against the base of the toy. I linger, watching the rhythm of her breathing as I coax her closer to the edge.

"Jessica?" I warn as she wiggles back and forth

trying to command more from me than I'm willing to give her in this moment.

"Please! Oh… God Please?"

Stopping all stimulation, I slap her bare arse "Count Jessie."

"One Sir." She struggles.

"One, Teasing Daddy comes with a price. Let's start again."

Picking the flogger up again, I strike her bare bottom again, this time she responds correctly. I pace the strikes out, taking time to tease with the tips of the flogger along her core. Having reached the midway point, I have her turnover, legs spread wide giving me full access to her tender clitoris.

I dip the handle of the flogger into her, applying pressure to her clit with my other hand, building her intense need once more.

"Stop, please, please?"

Ignoring her pleas, I continue to slide the handle in and out, her hips rolling with the action, bringing on my own need for satisfaction, with her pleading. I play with her until her begging turns into a purr.

"Bastard!" she cries as the real world of denial hits her again.

"Remind me, what's the count?"

I watch as she tries to regain focus before answering me "Five! Teasing Daddy… comes with a price, Sir."

I give her further time to cool down by wiping the handle of the flogger with her dixie shorts, the leather of the handle is damp with the remnants when I take aim again. This time I focus on her ripe pussy, hitting her over tender clit with an electrifying sting. Her count coming loudly at the intensity of the sensation. I repeat the action again and then don't allow her to finish the count before applying for another in the same spot. Shortening the gap with each strike I edge her to completion. Her orgasm quakes her against her will, I lay extras as it ripples over her.

"I'm sorry, I'm sorry, I'm sorry" She begs forgiveness for taking her fulfillment as she recovers. "Please…I…"

"Looks like we'll be starting over."

"Oh God! No! Please no! I'm sorry"

"This." I tap her wet pussy "Belongs." A second tap "To me." I tap again.

"Yes Sir, I… "

"So, we start again. The count is one, I don't cum without permission." I don't wait for a response, laying each strike once again over her tender spot, building and teasing. By the time we reach ten, tears are streaming down her cheeks.

Dropping the flogger, I release my manhood, taking position I ram myself to the hilt, then wait for her to adjust to my invasion, she's barely holding control over her desire to explode, as I begin to build towards my own completion.

Raising her legs over my shoulders, her bottom lifted from the mattress, allows me access to the plug, I plough into her, hitting the jewel with each invasion, pulling away giving her a moments reprieve. My pace and depth increase, Jess is purring unintelligibly as I close in on my own explosion.

"Cum with me little one, squeeze Daddy dry, baby." I growl as I come deep inside her. Her own ripping through her as I empty into her. Her muscles sucking me deeper, I pull the plug and another orgasm fills her on the back of the first. I still and wait for her to relax her inner core, I rock slowly as I soften inside her now, knowing that she is incapable of preventing her orgasms at this point.

"Don't you dare, little one." I caution as I build her up again. "I'll teach you to tease, Jessie." I edge her as she begs me to stop.

"You gonna tease me again?" I growl.

"NO! Please, Daddy? No! I need, Daddy Please."

"Cum Princess!" I exchange my member for my fingers now, and pull orgasm on top of orgasm, until she squirts over my hand.

She's glistening, totally wrung out when I finally pull my fingers from inside her, even that movement bringing ripples she's so sensitive.

"Relax, Jessie, I'll clean you."

"No more, please I won't tease, I'll be a good girl."

Wetting down a small hand towel with cold water from the tap, I return to find Jess asleep. Placing the towel over her precious, tender kitty kat, she stirs and purrs once more, I clean her tenderly, noting vibrations in her legs as her muscles react to the stimulation.

"Let's get you into the bed, Princess." Having folded the comforter back on one side of the bed, I lift her into place. Giving her forehead kisses as I tuck her in, sleep overtaking her fully.

"Sleep tight beautiful." Thinking how nice it would be if she was mine.

I shake the thought remembering her husband and family, she'd asked earlier how long I planned to keep her, in truth I wanted forever, but these moments between us have a history of being temporary, tomorrow she'll remember she hates me, tomorrow she'll fight me.

Jess

"LIZZY!" I wake up screaming, she's not far from here, an arm is wrapped painfully around my middle, he squeezes tighter in response to my outburst.

Last night's activity has left me tender and sore inside and out, and I seem to be wearing a large pad, oh! I think as I realize, he's put me in one of the pull ups he purchased yesterday, and from the weight of it below, I seemed to have soaked it somewhat.

"Ron? Let me up, please?" I know he's awake behind me, his breathing has changed. Thankfully he does, and I'm able to escape to the bathroom. I waste no time in removing the embarrassing underwear and tossing it in the bathroom bin. Ronald has set out clean towels, and the items he purchased from Boots are set out on the counter for me. I don't bother to latch the door but set about getting clean and refreshed.

When I return to the bedroom thirty minutes or more later, he's no longer here, he's set out a pair of jeans, a nice blouse and matching underwear. On his high-backed chair, he's set my new trainers and a pair of ankle socks. Grateful I get dressed, finish fixing my hair, throw on some perfume and deodorant.

With him still absent, I take a chance on being able to leave the room and find no one guarding the door, I make my way down the stairs and into the kitchen.

Ronald is mixing something in a bowl; he's bare from the waist up. Walking up behind him, I embrace

him placing a kiss on the back of his shoulder blade, my fingers tracing the snake that intertwines with the skull tattoo across his torso.

"Morning, Princess."

"What you making?"

"Breakfast. Go take a seat on the bench, I bring you some juice."

I don't want juice, but I'm too tender to complain, I hear him laugh when I hiss as I sit down. The bench doesn't have any cushioning relighting the punishment I've received by Tank and Ron's hands.

Ron sets a glass of orange juice in front of me, along with a container of pills, "The doctor will be here later, but he sent these ahead for you."

Nodding I take the pills with the juice, it's bitter and not something I normally drink, but I don't complain. Having downed the juice I ask for coffee, but get denied, he offers more juice, I request water, happily he agrees and sets a second glass, this one taller and with ice.

"Lizzy is close, we need to help her." I announce as he sets scrambled eggs and buttered toast in front of me. "She's not eating."

"Neither it seems, are you?"

Making a show of scooping up some egg, "It needs to be this morning for a good outcome" I mention before popping the spoon in my mouth.

Ron returns to the kitchen, I smell coffee moments later, looking over as I finish my toast, he's leaning against the counter observing me. I make a display of finishing the last bite and lick my lips slowly. He stalks over, leaning over my shoulder, he cages me in from behind.

"How quickly you forget, little Jess."

I giggle as he pulls my head back gently with a handful of hair, he's shaking his head, but a large smile is pinned across his face as he leans over and kisses the tip of my nose.

"You're writing checks, your sweet ass can't cash, girly."

"Mm, maybe." I grin in reply.

"Maybe you need to wear a little reminder this morning?"

"Nope! I don't think so." Comes my sassy retort.

"No?"

"Definitely, no Daddy, I'm still very sore."

"Better behave, then Princess." He gives me a forehead kiss, before releasing me. Just then a couple of the ladies that stayed over last night, come nattering into the kitchen. "Make yourself at home, and stay out of trouble, baby." Ron tells me, before leaving me to finish my water.

"Hey, would you like one?" One of the ladies offers me.

"I'm good." I say raising my half full glass of water.

The other lady swings herself over the bench next to me "I'm Cheryl, that's Linda, you sure you don't want coffee, sounded like you had a wild night?"

I shake my head, embarrassment flooding my face as I realize just how loud I'd been last night "Not allowed, but thanks." I grin.

"Leave her be Cheryl, Steve's grumpy enough without you stirring the pot!"

"So, you're with that arseh - I mean Steven?" I ask Linda.

"We both are, Cheryl." Responds for her.

"That tracks! Well ladies I'm sorry but unless you're under orders to watch me, I'm outta here!"

"Ouch!"

"Well? You minding or not ladies?"

"Not!" states Cheryl

Getting up, I leave the plate and glass on the table,

leaving the kitchen on a mission to explore my new prison. So far, I've seen the entrance area, the kitchen and the bedroom including the en suite, although its much smaller than I'd have if I was back home in the states.

The thought of home brings reality crashing back to me, I have to set Lizzy free and then hopefully I'd be allowed to go home. I miss my husband, the dogs and my job, I desire my freedom. Walking without really seeing the hallway I'm going down, I focus on the door at the end, out of the glass window, I can see the back lawn.

Opening the door without really processing my actions, I exit the house and entered the back area, the patio goes a few feet away from the house, before turning to grass. I keep on walking, no destination in mind. I'm picturing home, the pine trees, the heat, the humidity and sounds of home. I walk into the tree line at the end of the large lawn area, where I'd seen the wolves run last night. No snakes here, no killer spiders either I muse. The cool breeze points me deeper into the woods, my soul torn between the familiarity of this country and my home back in the States.

Tears threatened as my vision blurs, my heart twisting in confusion of the past, present and my unknown future. A wetness against my skin, disturbs my thoughts, looking down I'm greeted with the oversized silver wolf.

"I'm not running, just thinking and walking." I tell the wolf, reaching to run my fingers over his fur. The connection giving me his name "I promise Charley boy!"

Charles growls at my adjustment to his name, but I shrug and ignore him, beginning to walk away. I've not taken two steps, when I feel teeth around my wrist.

"Fine! Charles, let go of me." I look down at him as he decides to release my wrist I turn around and head back in the direction of the house. The wolf; Charles keeping pace at my side.

"It's not like have anywhere to run too, you know?" I grumble as we wander closer to the house. Coming back out of the trees, I see Steven approaching, just my luck I think as the wolf growls again, apparently, I'd stopped moving.

"Jeez! What's your rush?"

Meeting Steven halfway across the lawn, Charles takes off into the trees, leaving with the enemy.

Moments later, a man in beige shorts joins us.

"Thanks, Charles, this one has a tendency for disappearing."

"I wasn't running, Wanker! I was walking!" I spit at Steven, before storming off in the direction of the house once more.

"Ron wants you in the study!" Steven calls behind

me.

"I want's don't get!" I reply. I begin sprinting towards the open garage door to the side of the patio. I can hear a car engine running. Not much further, maybe I can take off and get some me-time, but instead I'm knocked forward and face plant just shy of the patio. Paws have me pinned and Charles is growling in my ear.

"Get off me Wolfie! Hasn't anyone told you not to play with Witches?" With that I send him an electrified reason to get off. He cries out in pain and jumps clear but is just as quickly back to prowl around me, as I start to sit up.

"That's against the rules, Jessica!" Comes Steven's condescending voice.

"Fuck off, Wanker!" I say as I dust myself off, and turn once more towards the house, the wolf nipping at my heels "Bite me, Wolfie, I dare you!"

Opening the door I used before, I reenter the hallway, suddenly aware, I have no idea where Ron's study is. So, I head up the stairs instead and into the bedroom, shutting the door before either Steven or Charles get the chance to join me. I twist the lock on the handle and head into the bathroom, locking that door behind me also. Closing the lid on the toilet, I take a hard seat, feeling the pain of the strips I'm still putting up with.

Fuck them all, I think as I pull on the ether and

heal myself, resolving myself to figuring out a way out of this and back home to my family.

I hear the commotion as Charles and Steven come crashing into the bedroom, "Jessica?" they call in unison.

"Get lost! I can't even take a fucking piss without you fuckers?" I scream at them through the still closed and locked bathroom door.

"I'll go get Ronald" I hear Charles say.

I hear his footsteps leave the room, as I relinquish this fight with Steven and unlatch the door, opening it wide, I stare back at him.

"Fine! You Win! Now what? Where's his fucking study? It's not like I received a map of my prison!"

"It's your funeral, keep digging." The smug git states folding his arms, leaning on the door frame to bathroom, effectively blocking my only exit.

I contemplate shocking him as well, but then a flash of the past reminds me that's probably not a good idea, shocking Charles earlier could be reasoned as self-defense, since he was in wolf form, but a straight attack towards Steven wouldn't end well for me.

I turn around, resume my previous position on the toilet, fold my arms and challenge the wanker with a childish but satisfying staring game.

"And you need to apologize to my ladies, especially my sweet Linda, I don't know what you said, but you hurt her feelings, Witch!”

I drop my eyes, replaying the conversation in my head, I'd not been nasty, what had they told him? I didn't think I'd said anything hurtful, they belonged to him, so they aren't gonna be friends of mine.

Pretty simple, really. I settle on "Whatever!" Just as Ron taps Steven on the shoulder, giving him the signal to leave.

Jess

"I should have known better, than to leave you alone, it's my fault, right Princess?"

Fuck! That's a trap my brain warns, I'd already locked eyes with Ron so it's too late to act submissive, and not knowing what lies Cheryl and Linda had already woven, puts me at a clear disadvantage. On top of that I've taken it upon myself to heal, staying mute is my best option.

"The doctor arrived early, he's waiting in my office, come on?"

Taking the escape, I take Ron's hand without complaint and allow him to guide me, we go back downstairs, turning to cross the entrance way into a hallway I'd not yet explored. Paying close attention, I'm creating my own mental map of the ground floor layout, third door on the left, turns out to be his office.

"Try to be a good girl for a change." He warns as he opens the door.

Walking in, a young man, dressed in a white

button shirt and grey trousers, walks over to greet me. "I'm Doc Danson, I've reviewed your medical history, and I've already prescribed the equivalent medications to your American ones. I'd like to do a basic physical and take some lab samples, if that's okay with you my dear?"

"I guess so." I shrug.

"That'll be great! Your case is an interesting one." He comments.

Ron takes a seat on the two-seater couch in the large room, as the doctor walks me over to the desk. He tells me to take a seat on the desktop.

I look over at Ron, who gives a nod, before hopping up and planting my rear on the desktop. The doc opts to get a blood sample first, it only takes him three strikes. Next, he takes temperature, pulse and blood pressure, all the basic stuff I'd come to expect of a new doctor on my case.

"Miss, I'm going to need you to get undressed" Doc announces.

I looked over at Ron, he nods. I give him a second look, which says really. But he just nods again.

Ron joins me noticing the change in my demeanor "Don't be shy, he's the doctor, Princess."

Not happy with Ron, I turned my attention to the Doctor "What exactly do you need to see?"

"I'm going to check your overall condition, then I'll do a breast exam and a vaginal exam. Nothing out of the ordinary, I promise you."

"No! I don't consent to any of it. You've pre-scribed the medications, thanks Doc, everything else can wait 'til I go home." I try to step around Ron, but he has me trapped between him and the large desk

"I'm serious Ron, no!"

"Doc, can you give us a moment, please."

"Sure"

Ron waits until the door closes behind the Doctor "What gives?" He still has me firmly trapped.

"I have a whole team of Doctors back home; I'm not looking for another."

"But you're not home, you're here, with me." Any sadness felt by his words quickly turn to rage as he continues "I'm trying to make sure you're okay while you're here with me."

"And just how long am I here? You didn't need me to be on location to rescue little Lizzy, so?"

"You're not here for Elizabeth." he confirms "You're here for..."

"You better not say you?"

"Jess, would that be so bad? You and I are made for each other, I can read you like an open book, your response to my touch is incredible." His words are undeniable, but so is the fact that our relationship is one built on toxic distrust, he is my bloody kryptonite. "Don't you lie to either of us,

Princess!"

"I love my husband."

"And?"

"And" frustration vibrates down our connection "I hate you! I'm fucking addicted to you! There you happy now, fucking control freak!"

"Take your clothes off, Little girl."

His command chills me with the calmness in his voice, his eyes daring me to refuse remind me of last night. Using one foot to free the other, I kick off the trainers before reaching for the button on the jeans. I'm grateful when he gives me room to bend over and free myself of them without his assistance. My fingers tremble with a mixture of rage and arousal as I unbutton the blouse I'm wearing.

"Bra and panties, Princess"

He has me standing completely naked with the exception of the cute, lace frilled ankle socks.

"Do a twirl baby, let me see."

"I fucking hate you!"

"I know you do, Girly" He's making the universal hand sign for me to turn around.

"So, this is what you've been hiding?" Ron halts my twirl grabbing a hold of my upper arm, he strikes me firmly on the clean canvas I'm now presenting him.

"No, I just don't like being poked and prodded by doctors in the buff!" I spit as I pull myself free, spinning

back to face him.

"Tell me, whose are these?" He grabs one of my breasts.

"Seriously?"

"Answer me." Pinching my nibble hard as he does.

"Yours."

"Turn that beautiful butt back around, Princess." Ron, immediately gives a folly of hard smacks on my rear, then grabs my now painful blooms "And these?"

"Yours." He's annoying me with his tired game of ownership.

"That's right, you belong to me, do you feel me in our connection as well?"

"You know I do."

"So, when I want to show your beauty to others, what will you do?"

"Whatever!"

The pain of a long sharp object catches my breath, as he sets a new line of fire across my arse, my hand flying back to defend the affected area. Ron grabs my wrist holding my arm outstretched behind me.

"Palm up!" It was a stupid reflex, he caught me off guard, whatever it is in his hand also being unexpectedly lethal "Jessica?" I turn my hand over, the next strike blazing across my open palm "Keep this out of my way." immediately balling my hand into a fist, trying to find relief, I snatch it free of his light hold.

Ron begins striking me with the foreign object again, I keep silent count while trying to decipher what he is wielding. It whistled slightly as he takes aim, and brings it across my skin, the contact a light thud. I burn to look over my shoulder to catch a glance, but the stripe across my palm still burns keeping me in position.

"Now, the Doctor is coming back in, and you will consent to his examination. Do you understand me?"

"Yes, Sir." My voice giving away the true extent of my pain.

"Turn around, Jessie" lifting myself from my position, I turn to see Ron closing an extended metal rod

"Who knew this lightweight pointer would work so nicely, think I'll keep this handy."

Leaning forward he kisses me before abandoning me for the study door, I place one arm across my breasts, the other is traveling cover my pussy. "Arms at your sides." He says without even looking over at me, my head drops in shame "Eyes on me, you're beautiful."

I'm so vulnerable as he opens the door fully, inviting the Doctor back into the room "Finish your examination doc."

The doctor asks questions about the symptoms I've previously reported, and then discusses the genetic findings he has seen in my record, all the while, he's touching me. My skin crawls, not because he's ugly, but because it's an invasion of my privacy. At least he doesn't make any comments when he sees the fresh marks on my rear.

Ron leaves me sitting on his desk, as he escorts the doctor out of the room, he must have walked him to his car given the time it takes for him to return "Can I get dressed now?" I request when he finally reappears.

"I like what you're wearing" Ron approaches pondering the idea of embarrassing me further "remind me Jessica, who do you belong too?"

"You, I belong to you, all of me is yours, Ron." I parrot bored with his repetition.

"And if I want you to remain as you are for the rest of the day, what will you do?"

Fuck! Would he really do that to me, I pull at the connection us, he seems to be toying with me, but he's shielding so I can't get a clear reading of his intentions. "As I'm told, but you can't punish me when your jealousy makes you angry. The wolf Charles has already had a taste of me, you can't get angry if eyes linger too long."

"How did he taste you?"

"He licked me! Nibbled my ankles and bit my

wrist tenderly."

"Did he? Show me that arse of yours."

"You sent him after me, you can't punish me for your mistake?"

"Can't I?" He's extending his new weapon again.

"No fair!" I pout, the idea of sticking my tongue out licking at the edge of my common sense.

"Maybe?" He reaches in close and steals a kiss "Turn around."

Ron

She's so beautiful when her little comes out to play, I can't resist stealing a kiss "Turn around." I softly growl our lips still so close. Her eyes drop and close as she summits, turning around in the tight space my body is providing.

I trail the pointer up the back of her legs, the little ball at the end of the pointer barely touching, damn I'm so lost to her. I feel down our connection, her rage has softened, she's enjoying the tenderness of the moment.

I give her a quick flick of my new toy on her exposed thighs, before returning to lightly caressing her with it. "I wish you would stay; you're submission is beautiful." I give her another tap lightly "Get dressed,Princess." Stepping away, I regret my words instantly, I want to give her so much more.

"Why am I here?" she asks pulling her jeans on.

My mobile phone chirps, saving me from her question, checking the notification its good news that I can share with her "They've got Elizabeth."

"I'm glad she's safe, but you haven't answered my question, why Ron?"

"They are going to bring her here, the two of you need to get to know one another, by all accounts you have a lot in common." I'm going to ignore the question as long as I can, last time Rubec was a part of the conversation, my Witch hadn't taken it well.

"So, you're not going to tell me?"

"You still need to apologize to Steve's ladies." I don't really care if she does or not, but it's a diversion from her persistence "You really hurt Linda, you know?"

"Then she needs thicker skin, if she's going to be his!" She has a point, and I can't help but grin at her annoyance.

"Play nice, Jessica!" I caution sternly.

"Fine, but only cause I don't want more of that thing!" She points at my new toy.

"Good to know, Princess."

She growls at me, as I take her hand and we go in search of Cheryl and Linda. Thankfully we don't have to go far, they are in the entrance area with the other members, waiting for the pack and our own guys to return.

Elizabeth

The hatch opens and closes behind me, I hear the trays slide in and out, I no longer feel hunger, my body has adjusted, I've not needed a bathroom break in two days, my wolf has gone very quiet, she's given up hope of persuading me to change the course of my actions.

It's a calm sense of acceptance deep inside of us both. The red light still blinks, but Rubec seems to have abandoned us. I know how cruel she can be, but now I no longer care, if I die today, I will have my release. I hope today is that day, I'm tired of surviving, I survived the attack that turned me so violently, I survived as a feral in a human world, I survived as he forced my return to his world, and I have been surviving here, alone in this box of silver.

I've been slipping in and out of consciousness, I no longer know day from night or night from day, the hatch opens, the hatch closes, I know nothing outside of that now, I'm no longer forced into the dirty toilet, to be observed taking care of basic needs.

No one is coming, I welcome death, will I see the angel coming I ponder, I no longer have the strength or will to adjust my form from this place where I lay. Please death take me I prayer, I wish I had the strength not to breath, but automatic functions are beyond my control.

Light disturbs my thoughts, voices undisguisable, far too loud, pain radiates as I float for a moment, is this death, has death come for me. Lights blinking on and off, I should open my eyes but it's already too painful through my closed lids.

Charles

The biker Witch says today will end well, but I know Elizabeth, she's stopped eating and drinking days ago, she will welcome death over submitting to the demon vampire queen. It hasn't even been that long since I had to send for outside help to save her from her death wish out in the desert.

With the biker club members making our pack numbers larger, we've already breached the outer security and entered the main floor of the house. Our intel suggesting Rubec hasn't been here in several days.

Rubec's human servants surrender quickly given the size of our pack, I grab a young male blood bag, forcing him to unlock the electronic doors into the basement. As we walk along the hall lights blink on overhead, with the common sound of long bulbs.

This hallway is slightly sloping downwards, as we round the corner, I note the sound of the bulbs going out behind us. I bloody hate vamps, entering the lower area before me, I see the common room, as expected it is furnished in the stereotypical gothic style, blood red velvet curtains covering doors, the cage in the center of the room, currently unoccupied has restraints attached to the outside corners.

"Where is she?" I growl at my hostage.

He's shaking his head "I…I don't…"

"Don't fucking lie, boy!" I let my wolf out just enough to warn this human twit not to play with me "One of you blood bags have been feeding her! Now which room?"For a blood bag he's gutless, his bladder releasing down his pant leg, as he points towards a curtain covered door.

I grab him by the scruff and push him ahead of me, if he's lying the vamp on the other side of the door will kill him first.

He taps in a code and the door clicks open, shoving him forward, his body opens the door, the light coming on with the action. Seeing Beth's unmoving body lying in the center of the cell, I toss the blood bag against the opposite wall, my wolf is happy to see he's unmoving as he lands in an awkward pile.

Elizabeth hasn't registered the invasion into her cell, this is bad. Scooping her carefully into my arms, Isaac's grey wolf circles us, signaling a clear exit. Beth is muttering to herself, as I follow Isaac out the way I came, I clearly hear her ask if I'm death.

"Hush, it's only me" I watch as she curls into my arms, I think the biker Witch might have left out important information "Shh, it's okay now."

With every light coming on as I once again walk the long hallway back up into the main house, I wince in tune with Beth's jerks. The bright light is obviously too much for her in her weakened condition.Entering the main floor, I'm grateful when one of the bikers places a blanket over her now trembling form.

Getting into the van, relief washes over me, the whole extraction went flawlessly and thankfully Beth is sleeping on my lap within minutes of us hitting the open road.

Charles

Jessica opens my door as we pull up in front of the club manor "Allow me?" I nod, pulling my wolf to the background.

"Hey Lizzy, here" the biker Witch moves the blanket aside, she takes Beth's hand "Lizzy? Take... She's shielding, can you wake her?" she turns to me and asks gently.

Obviously, my wolf is closer to the forefront than I intend.

"Jess, maybe we should let Charles take her inside first?"

I watch as the biker Witch seems torn between wanting to aid Beth and her guardian's request.

"Okay, but she..." Ronald assists her out of the car, whispering something into her ear, which sounds like

"I see it too."

My overwhelming need to care for Beth has my wolf refusing to relent, getting out of the van, I cradle Beth securely in my arms, grateful that my pack has warned the remaining bystanders to leave the area.

Walking into the main entrance, Ronald directs me into his office.

Closing the door behind, Ron takes the seat behind the desk, giving me plenty of space to settle on the two-seater couch. His Witch kneels at my feet, careful not to make eye contact, she requests for me to wake Beth.

"Angel of Death?"

"Yes, sweety, I'm here for you, but Lizzy it's not your time!"

The feisty biker Witch is being so gentle, one hand laying calmly on my thigh, I feel nothing but calm warmth in her presence, she is calming my wolf as well. The soft purr leaving my lips is unintentional and catches me by surprise.

"Lizzy, will you take my hand?" I watch dazed as waves of pure energy ease me towards sleep. The bike

Witch gently reaches in between my guarding arms, taking Beth's hand into her own. "Good girl, now Lizzy take what you desire, I'm sending you healing vibes."

"I'm ready for Death, won't you take me?"

"It's not your time Lizzy, besides Charles will not be happy with us, now take what I give you, bless us both with your healing, Goddess bless us both."

"So, mote it be." Beth responds resigned.

Beth's other hand reaching out now, taking the biker Witch's other hand, she frees me from the spell that Jessica had over me. Anger floods me, but it fades just as fast seeing the strength Beth is regaining through their connection.

"All better now, Lizzy?"

"Um, I'm hungry." Letting go of Jessica's hands now, Beth covers her stomach with her own.

"Food is on its way." Ronald states "Jess, let's leave them to it." Offering a hand, he escorts her out, just as food arrives, Isaac bringing in a tray of steak and chicken, along with a jug of water and two glasses.

"Who healed who?" Ron asks his Witch as he holds the door.

"Um, yes!" Her reply as the door closes behind them.

I shake my head in mild amusement before turning my attention to my own charge.